Returning His Love

Book 2 of the Unconditional Series

By Jacqueline Francis

First paperback edition July 2019

Book design by Romance Novel Covers Now

ISBN 978-1733679923 (paperback)
ISBN 978-1733679930 (ebook)

Books by Jacqueline Francis

Table of Contents

Dedication

To all of the lovely romance readers who I have met along the way—here's to never-ending happily ever afters!

And to the beautiful Z... may you always have an adventurous spirit.

Chapter 1

The voice over the loudspeaker announcing boarding flights was muffled as Madeline Danzer stood in Gate M12 at O'Hare International Airport in Chicago, her hand shaking as she dialed her sister's number.

There was absolutely no way that her sister would understand why she was at the airport at eight o'clock at night on New Year's Day with a passport in her hand.

Maddie leaned her tall, lithe body up against a wall, the noises of the busy airport keeping her company. She left town in the dark of the evening, feeling like a fugitive as she snuck away, leaving Willow Falls, Wisconsin, behind as she took an airport shuttle to Chicago.

Flipping her long blonde ponytail behind her shoulder, Maddie waited for her sister to pick up.

"Hey Mads, what's up?" Melissa answered a few seconds later.

"Hey sis. How's it going?" Maddie began cautiously. She could hear the barking of Melissa's new fiancé's dog in the background and Jakob telling him to quiet down.

"I'm fine. Happy New Year! What are you doing tonight?" Melissa asked, a smile in her voice.

"Promise you won't get mad?" Maddie asked hesitantly, biting her bottom lip. Her blue eyes stared down at the drab tile floor as she spoke, willing the words to come out easier.

"Okay," Melissa answered cautiously, her voice quick with concern. "What's going on, Mads? Where are you?"

"I'm at the airport in Chicago," Maddie began. "I'm about to board a flight to Scotland."

"What?" Melissa screeched. "You're joking, right?"

"I'm not," Maddie answered, her hands sweaty as she clutched her passport and boarding pass. The line for her flight was beginning to form, and she grew more and more anxious. "I had a once in a lifetime opportunity. I gotta go. Don't worry—Hazel is watching the apartment for me. I promise to explain more later. Love you!" Maddie spit everything out quickly, hanging up on her sister before she could answer any questions.

Powering her phone off, Maddie rushed over to the back of the line and attempted to not feel too guilty about deserting her sister with no warning, her bright yellow blouse and tailored jeans lightening up the dreary winter day.

For as long as she could remember, Maddie and

her sister had always stuck together through thick and thin. After their traumatic upbringing, they had finally been able to turn the page on the past and begin a new life. Lately, however, Maddie was feeling conflicted about her relationship with her sister.

Ever since Jakob King came into Melissa's life, their tight bond of sisterhood morphed into something very different. It was no longer just the two sisters against the world. Maddie was so happy for her sister, but also confused about her place in the midst of everything.

After scanning her boarding pass and walking onto the plane, Maddie slid into her seat and fiddled with the seatbelt. Stretching out her long legs, she gazed out the window and onto the tarmac as people around her got comfortable. It was Maddie's first time traveling internationally. She could not decide whether she was more nervous to meet Calum or to cross the ocean.

Two months earlier, it was a very ordinary day at Willow Falls Public Library when Maddie, the Assistant Director, sat at her desk during the lunch hour. As she munched on a slice of cold pizza, her eyes bulged while looking at a stack of new releases. Gracing the cover of a romance novel, Maddie set her sights on the most beautiful man in the entire world.

There, smack dab on the top of the pile of books stood a blond-haired, blue-eyed hunk of man shirtless in a blue and green checkered kilt on the cover of *Captivated by the Highland Laird*. Maddie began choking on the slice of pizza when she saw him, practically quivering at her desk.

Throwing the pizza down onto the desk, she picked up the paperback, pulling it close to her wide blue eyes. Maddie stared intently at the model, convinced she had never seen a more beautiful man. Trim and taut, the model stood on a rolling green hill, a castle in disrepair behind him. He stared out into the distance, a brooding look on his smooth face.

Less than ten minutes later, Maddie was able to use her research skills to find the name of the model. *Calum MacGregor*. Standing at 6'2", the thirty-year-old was a popular model in Scotland. After finding his Instagram and quickly following his account, she scrolled through the hundreds of pictures on his profile, most of them shirtless. His body was sleek, toned, and hairless. Maddie practically began drooling as she found herself liking all of his pictures, intently staring at the short video clips of him working out at the gym.

Laughing at herself for being so infatuated, Maddie scoffed as she saw that he had over 55,000 followers of his profile. Maddie's own Instagram, which mostly featured pictures of books she was reading, had a meager 353, most of which were spam bots.

That evening, she checked *Captivated by the Highland Laird* out from the library and devoured it in her quiet apartment. Taking a photograph of herself reading the book in bed with a wink, she posted it on Instagram and tagged Calum, doubtful that he would ever see it.

When she woke up the next morning, Maddie practically threw her phone when she saw that, not only had Calum liked her post, but he followed her back. She saw that he even messaged her, thanking her for tagging him in the cute photograph.

Maddie's heart would not go back to a normal pace. Before she knew it, she was messaging him back, flirting relentlessly. She was even more surprised when he replied back, continuing their conversation.

Before long, Maddie could not go anywhere without her phone. The harmless flirtation grew into something more and Maddie was smitten. While the six hour time difference was difficult, Calum had an odd work schedule so he often had lots of time to message Maddie when she was awake.

As much as she was embarrassed to admit it, Maddie spent hours staring at Calum's photographs, hardly believing that he was real. As time went on, the two began sending selfies to each other, his bright white smile lighting up her phone.

Maddie couldn't help but feel like this was a fairytale. What were the chances that, out of all of his followers, Calum chose her? He must have seen something special in her, and that made Maddie feel good about herself.

In their flirtations, Calum joked about Maddie coming to visit him in Glasgow. He wrote about all of the things he wanted to do there with Maddie, both in and out of the bedroom. Maddie was convinced that Calum was her Prince Charming.

Throwing caution to the wind, Maddie applied for a passport and talked to her boss about taking time off for a trip. After saving up her vacation time for nearly three years, this was her big chance at adventure. There was no way that she was giving up on the chance at love with Calum.

After packing her suitcase with warm winter clothes and sexy lingerie that she bought on a whim one day, Maddie was prepared for anything that her secret trip to Scotland would bring. Imagining Calum proposing to her on the moors, Maddie sighed contentedly as she thought about the possibility.

Before she left, her upstairs neighbor Hazel agreed to watch her apartment for her and retrieve her mail. Her online banking was already set up to automatically pay her bills, but she was glad to have Hazel just in case something unexpected came up. She also knew how much Hazel loved her big TV and on demand access to as many shows as she wanted.

While Maddie was leaving, the elderly but sassy Hazel scuttled into her apartment in her pink flannel nightgown and sat on her couch, reaching for the remote before Maddie could say goodbye.

As she waited for the plane to get ready to take off, Maddie could not stop thinking about Calum. Her heart was doing flip flops in her chest as the plane started down the runway. Looking at the middle aged woman sitting next to her, she smiled as they made eye contact. The heavyset redheaded woman clutched the armrests as the plane accelerated, gulping deeply.

"Are you nervous?" Maddie asked the woman.

"Aye," the woman replied. "I hate flying," she said, her thick Scottish accent coming out as her hands shook.

To distract her, Maddie began asking the woman about Scotland. Quickly, she found out that Gladys lived in Glasgow and was in Chicago to see her new granddaughter.

As Gladys talked about home, her grip on the armrests loosened and she began to relax. Maddie had the ability to make even the most uncomfortable person feel like everything was going to be okay. As the two sipped mediocre airplane coffee and talked about restaurants in Glasgow, the woman set her cup down and turned towards Maddie.

"And what are you going to Scotland for?" she asked, her dark eyes looking at Maddie inquisitively. It was Maddie's turn to grab the armrest as she decided to divulge her plans to the stranger with a kind, motherly face.

"Well, it's kind of a funny story," Maddie began, telling the woman how she met Calum and telling her plans to surprise him.

The woman grabbed her chest as Maddie told the story, her eyes opening wide as Maddie explained that she planned to surprise him by calling him from the airport.

"Oh dear God," Gladys said, making the sign of the cross. "You are a brave girl! And what does your mother have to say about all this?" she asked.

Giving her a sad smile, Maddie said, "My parents are actually no longer with us."

With a pained look on her face, Gladys reached out and grabbed Maddie's hand. "You poor thing!" she said. Before Maddie knew what the woman was up to, Gladys pulled out a pad of paper and a pen from her purse. "This is my phone number and my address. I live right outside the city. If you need anything, you come over, day or night, dearie. You promise?"

Smiling as she took the piece of paper from Gladys, Maddie tucked it into her bag and sat back, enjoying the quiet of the flight. Gladys pulled out a book, and Maddie almost choked when she saw that it was a copy of *Captivated by the Highland Laird*.

"You're not going to believe this, Gladys," Maddie said, interrupting the woman who was smoothing out a dog-eared page. "That's him. That's Calum."

Glancing down at the cover then back up at Maddie, Gladys let out a squeal. "Is this a bloody joke?" She asked. "What a handsome lad! A wee bit skinny but nothing that a few pots of stew won't fix. You're a lucky girl," Gladys continued, her eyes glued to the cover with Calum.

Smiling, Maddie nodded. "I know it," she said, feeling very happy with herself.

"Well I suppose I won't be offended if you don't call me," Gladys said. "Looks like you might be preoccupied," she continued, giving Maddie a knowing look.

Blushing, Maddie pulled out her Kindle and got lost in a book, trying to put the nervous jitters behind her. Although it took her a while to get into the romance novel she was reading, Maddie was quickly immersed in a world of cotillions and puffy dresses, of intrigue and romance.

After a thirteen hour flight, Maddie was exhausted. The time difference did not help things either, touching down in London at three in the afternoon the next day. She was able to sleep a bit with Gladys snoring quietly next to her, but all Maddie wanted to do was take a shower and slide into a cozy bed.

The two ladies caught the connecting flight to Glasgow after a short layover. Maddie was thankful for the time to get a coffee and freshen up a bit. Less than two hours later, the women touched down in Glasgow. She was finally here, finally in Scotland.

Waiting for her luggage at the baggage claim, Gladys came up to Maddie and gave her a big hug, wishing her the best. "Don't forget to call me if you need me," Gladys said, giving Maddie a squeeze.

"Thanks, Gladys," Maddie said, glad to have a friend in Scotland. As she grabbed her bag, Maddie passed the airport bookstore, where a huge display of *Captivated by the Highland Laird* books greeted her. Next to the display was a large, oversize cardboard cutout of Calum in his kilt.

Laughing, Maddie smoothed her hair as she leaned in to take a selfie with him. Knowing this was the perfect way to surprise Calum, she sent the picture to Calum and said, "Guess where?"

Moments later, Calum responded with a question mark.

"Glasgow airport :)" Maddie replied.

"What?" he replied, clearly confused.

"I'm here!" Maddie said. "Surprise!!" A minute passed before Calum wrote back. Maddie's heart began to beat faster as she waited for him to respond.

"Cool. What for?" Calum wrote. Heart falling deep into her stomach, Maddie tried not to be sad at his less-than-enthusiastic reply.

"You..." Maddie replied, knowing that now was not the time to play it cool.

"Wow!" Calum typed back. "Babe, I'm honored. I'm on set for a shoot right now. Why don't we meet at the pub later? O'Shaughnessy's. Right downtown, you can't miss it. Can't wait." Maddie let out a sigh of relief. Phew. Everything was fine!

For a second, she was worried that Calum did not want her there, and that terrified her! How embarrassed she would be to board a flight right back home, wasting all of her savings for nothing.

Gathering up her luggage, Maddie pulled her jacket tight and went out into the chilly Scotland air. Other than the accents around her, everything seemed pretty much like America. She didn't know why, but whenever Maddie thought about other countries, she just assumed that life would be radically different.

Shaking her head at her overactive imagination, Maddie stepped into a cab and asked to be taken to O'Shaughnessy's. She felt off-balance driving on the opposite side of the road at first, but eventually was looking out the window so much that it did not matter to her.

Although she was exhausted, Maddie was fascinated by the architecture of Glasgow. There were dozens of small shops built into light brown brick buildings and winding streets filled with people. She had never seen so many old buildings in one place. While it was dreary and chilly outside, there was no snow on the ground. Glasgow was *nothing* like Milwaukee, and that made Maddie's heart skip a beat in excitement. She lived for adventure.

As they crossed the River Clyde, Maddie stared at the SEC Armadillo, a silver auditorium that looked much like the Sydney Opera House. She could hardly contain her excitement as they neared the city center.

Slowly, the cab pulled to a stop on a small side street in downtown Glasgow. The businesses were lit up in the dim afternoon, the sun beginning to set. Outside her window was O'Shaughnessy's, which looked no different from a typical Wisconsin dive bar. Next to the pub was a coffee shop, with multiple floors of what appeared to be flats above all of the shops on the block.

After thanking the driver and tipping him,

Maddie pulled her luggage to the door of the pub. It appeared to be quiet before the after work rush, and she was glad to have some time to gather her thoughts before finally meeting Calum.

Opening the red door to the pub, Maddie was hit by the smell of fried food. Soft rock music played in the background. It was dimly lit inside. The old two men sitting at the bar turned to look in her direction. Not recognizing her, they turned their backs to her and continued nursing their beers.

Maddie walked up to the old wooden bar, wheeling her suitcase next to her. Unzipping her black jacket, she took a seat on a padded barstool and waited for the server. She checked her phone to see if Calum messaged her, but had no updates. She then checked her email and saw five emails from Melissa, demanding details about why she was in Scotland.

Maddie sent her a quick email, telling her that she would explain everything soon, and letting her know that she landed safely in Scotland. Slipping her phone in her pocket, Maddie looked up when she heard a scuffle behind the bar.

Stepping out from a back room, a tall, giant beefcake of a man hefted a keg over his shoulder. He came in front of her and practically threw the keg on the ground behind the bar, breathing heavily.

When he stood at his full height, Maddie took in his tall, muscled body. Wearing a black and red flannel shirt and a pair of jeans, the man had a scruffy light brown beard, practically golden in the neon lights behind the bar.

As his eyes roamed across her body, Maddie's face heated up. What was this brute of a man looking at?

Slowly, he began to roll the sleeves of his flannel shirt up, exposing the tattoos on his hairy arms. Maddie couldn't deny that he was an attractive man, but not her type at all. She went for men like Calum who were polished and clean-cut. The beast who was eyeing her up looked like he hadn't shaved in two weeks.

The man's piercing blue eyes were dark as he looked at her, and she could have sworn they got darker by the second. Breathing heavily, he walked up to Maddie behind the bar, set out a glass, and said, "What can I get you, love?"

Chapter 2

"I'll take a beer, whatever is your favorite," Maddie said. "And the juiciest burger you've got," she continued, her purple-manicured fingernails pushing wisps of her straight blonde hair behind her shoulder.

The bartender poured her a pint of Old Norway and set it in front of her with a nod, then strode to the kitchen door, grabbing a white apron from a hook.

Through the window into the kitchen, Maddie watched the man prepare her food for her, the burger sizzling on the grill. After taking a long gulp of the amber beer and then another because it was so delicious, she looked up again and found the man's blue eyes on her. He quickly looked down, and Maddie could have sworn he was blushing.

Maddie rubbed her thumb along the glass, willing herself not to look up at the man again. Losing her internal battle, she glanced up once more. The man was tall and burly, strong enough to lift an entire keg over his shoulders with no problem. She saw tattoos smattering his large forearms, their shadows bringing a bit of darkness to his facade. His beard was caramel-colored and scruffy, with hints of gray here and there. He was a handsome man, Maddie mused, but definitely too much of a bad boy for her liking.

Maddie enjoyed clean cut gentlemen like Calum, with smooth skin that coincided just right with a suit and tie. Bad boys weren't her type at all. They were too risky, too dangerous. She was more into Prince Charming than the Beast.

She could feel the warmth from the beer come over her body, and Maddie allowed herself to sit back and take in the atmosphere of the pub. Calum would be arriving any minute, and she was so excited to finally see him in person for the first time.

Maddie listened to the old men sitting next to her discuss sports, and diligently tried to get used to their heavy accents. It would certainly take some getting used to. Before she knew it, the bartender was sliding a plate in front of her.

Her mouth watered as she gazed at the juicy cheeseburger, cheese pouring out of the bun as fries surrounded it. Looking up at the bartender, she could have sworn he was a saint.

"You have no idea how much I need this," Maddie said, reaching for a fry and biting into it. She sighed contentedly as she tasted it, not realizing how famished she was from the travel.

"Long day?" The man asked, his eyes narrowing in on Maddie as she listened to her speak.

"Lots of travel," Maddie replied, taking a sip of her beer before picking up the enormous burger.

"Where are you from?" he questioned, his accent growing thicker the more Maddie heard him speak. *You* sounded more like *ye*. The accent was stronger than Calum's, but she could still decipher what he was saying.

"The States," Maddie replied, her mouth full of food.

"A wee bit from home," he murmured, wiping down the bar, desperate for something to do with his hands.

"I'm meeting my boyfriend here," Maddie replied confidently, sitting up a little straighter.

"Oh? Is he a local?" the man replied, tossing the towel down and looking intently at Maddie.

"Yes he is," Maddie blushed, thinking about seeing Calum for the first time.

"Lucky man," the bartender said quietly. "You need anything else, you holler," he told her as he walked down to the men to refill their pints.

Maddie devoured the food, pretending to pay attention to the football match on the television. She checked the ringer on her phone multiple times, making sure that it was on. It was.

Time went by and she heard nothing from Calum. First fifteen minutes, then twenty. She held out her glass and the man looked up at Maddie. He nodded and quickly refilled it with another beer.

She tried not to jump every time she heard people walking past the bar, hoping that it was Calum. Groups of people went past the window, but Calum did not. The bar remained deserted other than the men, and

Maddie wondered where everybody was going if they weren't out drinking.

"Are you coming?" Maddie texted Calum, hoping for a quick reply. Ten more minutes went by before she heard her phone ping.

"I got held up at work," Calum replied. "I will be by later. Sorry," the message said. With a sigh, Maddie leaned forward, resting her head on her hand and perching on the bar stool. She was exhausted and just wanted to see Calum.

As the minutes went by, Maddie became fascinated with watching the bartender work. He was meticulous in all of his motions. He did not just place cash in the register, he slid it in, being careful when pulling out the exact amount of change. Maddie leaned forward on the bar, cupping her hand. For a moment, just a moment, she shut her eyes and let herself take the experience in.

She could hardly believe that she was here in Scotland and slightly shocked that she had never been out of the country before. She had to admit that, for as adventurous as she was, this definitely took the cake.

Maddie had never really dated before. Sure, she met guys in college and had gone out for drinks, but things always ended up being more friendly than anything. At twenty-six years old, she felt pretty pathetic that she had never even had a real boyfriend. There were dozens of men that she had been interested in over the years who ended up going out with other women or not really giving her a shot. It wasn't that Maddie didn't put herself out there, but things never quite panned out.

How she longed for the romance in the novels that she read. How she wished that her life was like the fairy tales she devoured as a child. Maddie was young when she realized that things were not going to turn out the way they did in her storybooks.

With her traumatic family life, Maddie used reading as an escape, even if just for a few hours, from the world around her. After surviving an abusive father, Maddie was not sure that she would ever come to terms with the fact that they only way she and her sister were able to escape him was through the death—the murder —of her mother.

Knowing that her father was a murderer was something that Maddie tried not to think about too often. She found relief in the fact that he was now dead, too, but her M.O. was to avoid thinking about it and keep moving on in life.

Although she knew she was being adventurous and potentially irrational, booking a flight to Scotland to meet the one man who had managed to captivate her attention so strongly made Maddie practically giddy. She had never been so attracted to someone in her life, and could only fantasize about what it would be like to have such a beautiful lover.

Calum was everything she thought that she ever wanted in a man. She was a goner for his trim physique and smooth skin. She had always had a thing for blondies after swooning over some blond boy band singer when she was child, and Calum certainly fit the bill. It wasn't that Maddie really cared about what people looked like either way, but ever since crushing on Mr. Boy Band himself, there was no turning back from skinny blonds.

The noise of the people around her dwindled as she continued to daydream about Calum. She wondered what his skin would feel like, what it would be like to finally be in his arms, even what sexy masculine cologne he would wear.

Her phone dinged and Maddie bounced up in a start, not realizing that she had practically dozed off in the middle of a bar.

Looking up, she saw the bartender wiping a glass, smiling at her. He quickly looked away when she spotted him. Was that a blush she saw creeping up again? Ignoring it, she looked towards her phone which was perched next to her half-empty beer.

A notification told her that Calum had recently posted to Instagram. Quickly typing in her password, she opened up the app. Maddie scrolled through the app and found the new post. It was a heavily filtered picture of Calum standing in a studio between three women, scantily clad in bikinis. Calum had his arms around the women, wearing a pair of black skinny jeans and a flannel shirt. His hair was perfectly coiffed.

Maddie read the caption of the photograph. "Had a lovely day at a photo shoot with these beauties. Looking forward to a fun night." He tagged the models, who Maddie admitted were absolutely stunning.

Wow. She tried not to be hurt but it was very clear that Calum had priorities that did not involve her. She swallowed deeply and took a swig of the beer. She was exhausted.

Maddie stood up to stretch her legs, taking a look at the people in the bar. The older people were glued to the television, watching soccer—or as they termed it, football. The crowd occasionally cheered, then groaned, then cheered again.

Maddie stood with her beer, watching the television and fascinated with the game. While she was not a sports fan by any means, she enjoyed learning about new things and would take the opportunity to explore any thing new or different to her. She was a naturally curious woman.

After the game ended, with Glasgow winning, the crowd began to dissipate. It was nine o'clock and Maddie was shocked that the bar was completely empty once more. She assumed it would be rocking into the early morning, but all that was left were tables of empty beer mugs.

The bartender walked up to Maddie as she slid into a booth, not able to hide the sad look on her face. "Where's your man?" he asked in a heavy accent.

"He got held up at work," Maddie said confidently. "He will be here."

With a quiet nod, the man continued collecting the glasses and taking them behind the bar.

"Where is everybody?" Maddie asked, wondering why the place was empty.

The man said nothing, but nodded out the window to a pub across the street, which had huge floor-to-ceiling glass windows. Crowds of young people danced and drank, and as Maddie walked over to the small window in O'Shaughnessy's, she could hear the loud pop music from across the street.

"I see," Maddie said, understanding why the dark, quiet pub that she was in now was not exactly the most popular place to be when a swanky bar with a huge dance floor was right across the street.

"We usually end up closing around ten because nobody comes in," the man said, coming up to stand behind her and look outside the window.

"What's your name?" he asked, his Scottish brogue still strong, his voice deep.

She looked up at the bartender standing next to her. He was practically a behemoth compared to her, the sleeves on his flannel falling tight against his muscles.

"Maddie," she said quietly, gazing into his deep blue eyes. "What's yours?" she returned.

"Nick," the man replied. "Nick O'Shaughnessy." He stuck a hand out in front of him. Breaking his gaze, Maddie looked down at his hand. She reached out to grab it, and nearly gasped as she made contact. His big hand was rough and callused. The dim lights shed a bit of light on the scars that riddled his hands. Breaking the handshake, Maddie pulled her hand away, shocked at how she felt when she touched him.

She smoothed her hair with her hand, desperate to do anything but think about touching him.

"It's nice to meet you, Nick," Maddie said confidently. "If you don't mind, I'll wait here a bit a longer in case my boyfriend shows up," she said.

"Of course," Nick nodded. "I hope he comes."

Maddie threw some bills on the bar, then gathered her suitcase and jacket and took a seat in a booth while Nick busied himself putting stools on top of the tables. The quiet rock music playing in the background was comforting to Maddie, and she felt cozy in the booth.

"Whereabouts are you from in the States?" Nick asked, his deep voice sounding loud in the empty bar.

"Wisconsin," Maddie said, sighing with a smile. She talked lovingly about the great cheese and the fields that went on for miles. Nick stopped at a nearby table, holding empty mugs and nodding as she spoke.

Before she could stop herself, Maddie felt her head drifting onto her arms as she set them against the table. She began to fall asleep, the jet lag finally getting to her. Her hair fell against the table as she leaned down, telling herself that she would just rest her eyes for a bit until Calum came.

"Hey Maddie," a deep quiet voice said, lulling her out of sleep.

"Calum!" Maddie said with a start, throwing her head up and clearing the sleep out of her eyes. As she looked towards the voice, her heart fell as she saw Nick standing over her.

"Sorry," he said, sensing her disappointment. "It's just me."

"Oh," Maddie said. "What time is it?"

"Midnight," Nick said. "I stayed open because I hoped your friend was coming, but nobody has showed up."

"He must have gotten busy," Maddie said, trying to reassure herself as she grabbed her phone. There were no new notifications.

"Where are you staying?" Nick asked, sliding into the booth across from her, a bar towel tossed across his shoulder.

"Nowhere," Maddie said. "I figured I would have somewhere to stay." The dollar signs began calculating in her head as she thought about having to pay for a hotel room. She already cleared out her savings to buy her plane ticket, and had money set aside for sightseeing, but had not budgeted a hotel room. She was planning on staying with Calum.

"Do you know a good hotel around here? The cheaper the better," Maddie said, being completely honest with Nick.

"You're not going to find a hotel room around here this time of year," Nick explained. "The football championship is this weekend. Everywhere is booked up." Then his eyes lit up with an idea. "I have a place you can stay, though."

Maddie scoffed. "Listen, Nick, you're a nice guy and all but I'm not going to come home with you!" she exclaimed, as if being propositioned was the most ridiculous thing she had ever heard.

"Not *my* house," Nick clarified, blushing. "My sister just moved out of her flat upstairs, and all the furniture is still there. I live on the top floor. You would have the whole flat to yourself. After all, it's just for one night," he explained.

"How much would you charge?" Maddie asked, her interest piqued.

"250 pounds a night sound good to you?" Nick asked, cocking his head to the side.

Maddie's blue eyes grew wide as she took in the offer. "That must be *some* flat!" she exclaimed, trying to figure out how she could afford it.

A dimple appeared on Nick's cheek as he smiled, "I'm just fookin' with you, Maddie. You're thousands of miles from home. I won't charge a thing."

Maddie didn't know whether to laugh at the way Nick swore or to get excited about having some place to sleep. Maddie jumped up from the booth. "Seriously?" she squealed. "That would be amazing!"

Nick slid out of the booth and stood in front of her. She jumped forward and put her arms around his neck, wrapping him up in a hug. He stiffened as she came close, awkwardly patting her back as she squeezed him tighter. "You're the best!" Maddie said, excitedly. "I don't know how I'll ever repay you."

Looking down at her as she pulled away and gathered up her things, Nick reached out to grab her suitcase and said, "Knowing that you will have someplace safe to sleep tonight will be payment enough. Let's go, lass," he continued, wheeling her suitcase through the bar and heading through the back door to a staircase.

Maddie walked behind him, exhaustion beginning to hit her. As they made it to the second floor landing up old wooden stairs, Nick unlocked a door. After flipping on the lights, Maddie was surprised to see a contemporary flat. She was not expecting the sleek, modern wooden furniture and decorations in such an old building. White walls held contemporary art pieces. Two white chaise lounges were perched in front of a large television. A queen size bed with pink bedding was off to the side. Light, airy curtains graced the windows.

Stainless steel, top-of-the-line appliances were in the kitchen. It was a beautiful space. "Wow," Maddie said as she looked around. "This is amazing! You sure you don't mind that I stay here? What about your sister? All of her stuff is still here."

"Rosie took all of her clothes and things. I still have to bring her the rest of it. She moved to Inverness to be with her fiancé. Everything that's still in here are things she doesn't need anymore other than some pieces of art and knickknacks," Nick explained, wheeling her suitcase into the bedroom area, then coming back out.

"Well, words can't describe how grateful I am," Maddie said sincerely. "It really means a lot, Nick. You're my first friend in Scotland." Thinking about it, Maddie corrected herself. "Actually you're my second. I made friends with the sweetest lady on the flight here. If you two are any indication of what Scottish people are like, I think I'm going to enjoy my time here." Standing up, Maddie stifled a yawn as she walked over to Nick and gave him another hug.

He grunted as she squeezed him tightly. Pulling backwards, he broke off the hug and handed her a key. "Take this," Nick said. "In case you need it," he said, setting the key in Maddie's hand and closing her fingers around it.

"Thanks," Maddie said. "But I should only need to stay here the night. I am sure Calum will come tomorrow," she said, assuring herself.

"Yeah," Nick said quietly. "I bet." He walked to the door, and nodded at the deadbolts. "You be sure to lock up behind you, okay?"

"Got it," Maddie whispered. "Thanks again."

"Sweet dreams," Nick said quietly as he pulled the door closed, the hint of light from the hallway illuminating the tattoos on his forearms.

Maddie sighed as she walked to the door and locked up afterwards, like Nick had said. She could hear him climb the stairs to the third floor.

Before she could even begin to get upset about Calum or worry about why he didn't come to see her, Maddie slid off her boots and dug out a cozy t-shirt from her suitcase. Stripping off her clothes, which were grubby from travel, she threw the shirt over her head and crawled under the covers of the bed.

A sigh of relief escaped her mouth as her head hit the pillow. Maddie was convinced that she had never been in such a comfortable bed. She pulled the covers up over her, the down comforter cocooning her. With one last sigh of contentment, Maddie fell asleep, letting herself go into a deep slumber. Just like Scarlett O'Hara always said, tomorrow was indeed another day.

Returning His Love

Chapter 3

A quiet knocking stirred Maddie out of sleep. She stretched her long body out in the bed and rubbed the sleep out of her eyes. When she finally opened her eyes and saw the sun pouring into the flat, she remembered everything that happened the night before. With a groan, Maddie slid out of bed. The knocking continued, and she padded to the door.

Looking through the peephole, she saw Nick standing outside. She unlocked the door and pulled it open, happy to see a familiar face.

"Good morning, Nick!" Maddie said, feeling infinitely better after catching up on sleep.

"Afternoon," Nick said, his eyes roaming up and down Maddie's body.

"Afternoon?" she asked, oblivious that Nick was so captivated with her attire.

"It's 12:30," he said, smiling.

"Wow! I must have really needed the rest," Maddie said, yawning. As she stretched, the oversized t-shirt rode up her thighs, and she remembered that she wasn't really wearing clothes.

"Oh gosh," Maddie said, laughing. "I forgot I wasn't wearing pants!" She ran into the apartment and grabbed a blanket from the couch, wrapping it around her body.

With a grunt, Nick walked inside and set down a tray. It had a carafe of coffee and a plate of eggs, bacon, and a muffin. "I figured you might be hungry."

"To be honest with you, Nick," Maddie said as she sat down at the breakfast bar and gazed lovingly at the feast of food, "I'm fucking famished."

Nick smiled as Maddie picked up her fork and began eating the food, still hungry even after her big dinner last night.

"Did you make this?" Maddie asked after taking a swig of coffee.

"Yeah, downstairs," Nick said.

"Good gravy! You must get all the ladies," Maddie giggled.

"Sure," Nick said sarcastically. "So have you heard from that boyfriend of yours?" he asked, his eyes narrowing.

Shocked at herself for not even thinking to check her phone for news from Calum, Maddie jumped up from the stool and ran into the bedroom, dragging the blanket around her hips with her.

Finding her phone in the pile of covers, she saw that Calum had texted her an hour ago. "Sorry about last night. Got caught up with work. Let's go out for a drink today?" Calum asked her, a wink at the end of his text.

Maddie smiled wide and quickly replied back, asking him when and where they should meet. Dropping the phone back on the bed, she walked back into the kitchen, passing a wall with a full-length mirror on it. Maddie paled as she took in her sight. She had mascara clouding her eyes, looking like a raccoon. Her hair was frizzy and stuck up in a million places. Grimacing, she tried to smooth it out before walking back to the kitchen.

As she sat back down, she could feel Nick's gaze on her. "We are going out later," Maddie said, scooping a forkful of eggs into her mouth.

"So is he going to show up this time?" He asked gruffly, sipping on a cup of coffee as he stood in the kitchen, eyes not leaving Maddie.

"It was just a misunderstanding," Maddie asserted. "I couldn't expect Calum to drop everything just because I decided to surprise him. He's a very important model, you know," she said matter-of-factly before biting into the muffin.

"Wait," Nick said, coming towards the counter and setting down his coffee cup. "You're not talking about Calum MacGregor, are you?" he asked incredulously.

"I am," Maddie said, sighing with contentment as she thought about the beautiful, handsome Calum. "We haven't actually met yet," she admitted. "We met on Instagram."

"That fookin' shite!" Nick practically roared. He began pacing around the kitchen, muttering to himself.

"Do you know him? What's the deal?" Maddie asked as she leaned back on the stool, watching him as he paced around.

"Calum is well known in this town. Maddie, please, you have to listen to me," Nick said, walking closer to her, his Adam's apple bobbing as he stormed over to her, another tight flannel on again, today's colors being green and cream. "Be careful with him," Nick said. "He's not really known for being a one woman kind of man."

"I understand," Maddie said. "I've seen the thousands of women he has following him on social media. But I think things are different now," she explained, feeling good about her choices.

Nick looked at Maddie incredulously, as if she was telling him the sky was green and the grass was blue. "Maddie, please," he said, "just take it slow."

"Deal," Maddie said, finishing her coffee and gazing at Nick. She knew that she was playing with fire by falling for a famous model, but it was a risk that she was willing to take for love.

"So, do you own the bar? I noticed you have the same name," she said, changing the subject.

"Yes," Nick said. "It was my great-grandfather's."

"That's so cool!" Maddie said. "Do you run it full time or do anything else?"

"I do carpentry work as well," Nick said, his dark blue eyes seeming to get even darker as Maddie kept eye contact with him.

"That's awesome," she said. "I'm a librarian back home."

"Wow. Pretty *and* smart," he smiled. Maddie blushed at Nick's compliment, but knew he was just saying it to be kind.

"That's nice of you to say," Maddie said, smiling. Standing up, Maddie pulled the seam of her t-shirt down as she kept the blanket wrapped around her waist. "Thank you for breakfast," she said. "I should get ready now."

"I'll be downstairs when you leave," Nick asked. "Where are you meeting him? Do you need anything?" Maddie walked over to her phone, and saw that Calum asked to meet at O'Shaughnessy's again at 2:30.

"It looks like we are meeting at your bar," Maddie said, typing back a reply. "If I am not careful, your bar is the only bit of Scotland I'll get a chance to see!" she exclaimed.

"I'd make sure you get to see whatever you'd like," Nick said gently, picking up the tray of plates and walking to her door. "I'll see you soon," he said quietly.

"Thanks, Nick. You're the best!" Maddie called out as she walked into the bathroom. Her heart fluttered as she saw the enormous rain shower. She pulled the shirt over her head and tossed it on the floor. She strode her trim body to the shower and turned it on, letting steam fill the room.

After gathering her toiletries from her suitcase, she stepped into the luxurious shower. She stood under the stream for a long time, just thinking about her life. She was so excited to meet Calum and had to look her best. She spent a great deal of time shaving her legs, making sure she looked hairless and perfect for him. Everything was riding on him liking her in person.

Maddie would fervently deny to anyone that she overthought things and then overthink that, too.

Finally dragging herself out of the shower, Maddie dried and straightened her hair, her blonde locks cascading onto her shoulders. She applied her make-up, turning her face from side to side to make sure she looked good from every angle.

Maddie pulled out a creamy cable-knit sweater dress and a pair of leggings from her suitcase. She quickly dressed, realizing that she spent too much time on her hair and makeup. She slid on a pair of heeled grey boots and took a look in the mirror. With a quick swipe of chapstick on her lips, Maddie smiled as she walked towards the door, preparing herself to meet the love of her life.

Maddie strode down the stairs to the pub. She could hear Sam Smith playing over the speakers. As she walked through the back door into the pub, she heard Nick laughing. A redhead sat at the bar, a fruity drink in her hand. The woman was *literally* twirling her long hair around a finger as she talked to Nick. He laughed with her as he filled and then poured a drink from a shaker. A girlfriend perhaps?

Maddie looked around, nervously awaiting Calum. She looked back over at the bar and found Nick watching her. She smiled and winked at him, then sat at a booth, absentmindedly tapping her fingers against the table. She pulled out her phone and snapped a few pictures of the bar. Sending them in an email to Melissa, she wrote about how dive bars look the same everywhere. Maddie began to tap her fingers on the table. Her nerves were getting to her.

Nick slid a beer in front of her. "Liquid courage," he said to her, a wry smile on his face.

"Thanks. I need it," Maddie said, taking a long gulp of the beer. He went back behind the bar, helping out the two people who were lingering about.

Moments later, the door to the pub swung open and Maddie nearly screamed. With a yelp, she stood up and ran to Calum, who was dressed in a smart peacoat and skinny jeans. On his head, he wore a red beanie, his blond hair poking out from underneath it.

Calum reached out to hug Maddie, his eyes wide as she darted for him. He carried a single red rose in his hand. Pulling Maddie into an embrace, he grabbed her face and kissed her in the middle of the bar.

"It's really you!" Maddie said once they broke the kiss. "I can't believe you're real."

Calum looked just like his photographs. He was tall and skinny, but had small muscles. His skin was smooth and hairless, and his chiseled face was so attractive to Maddie. She could hardly believe that the man she dreamed about for so long was really standing right in front of her, and he just kissed her to boot!

Handing Maddie the rose, Calum said, "I'm so excited that you are here." His accent was lighter than Nick's, his voice not as deep. "You really surprised me when you told me you were here."

"It was supposed to be a surprise," Maddie said, stepping back to take him all in. "Are you happy?" she asked nervously.

"Of course, babe," Calum said, leaning in to kiss Maddie on the forehead. "What do you say we get a drink?"

Smiling she walked over to the booth she was sitting at, Calum following close behind her. After she slid into the booth, Calum found a spot next to her, opting to not sit across from her.

Nick barged out from behind the bar and strode over, a scowl on his face.

"Hey mate," Calum said as Nick came over. "Long time no see."

"Likewise," Nick grunted out. He had his flannel sleeves rolled up again today, and Maddie could begin to make out some of the tattoos on his forearms. She saw flames and what looked like a family crest.

"I'll take a vodka and soda, with SkinnyGirl vodka if you have it," Calum said. With a snort, Nick shook his head and strode behind the bar, preparing the drink.

Calum looked towards Maddie as she touched the petals of the rose he gave her. "I can't believe you're here," Calum said. "I'm sorry I didn't see you last night. What did you end up doing?" he asked.

"I went to bed," Maddie said. "It was good to get some sleep after traveling. What about you?"

"I had a, uh, work event," Calum said. "I didn't get a chance to be on my phone much."

"Sure, I get it," Maddie nodded, putting the Instagram post out of her mind. "Work is work," she smiled, giving him the benefit of the doubt.

She could hardly believe that she was inches away from *the* Calum MacGregor! If she wasn't so focused on trying to keep her cool and acting suave, she would positively swoon. He looked better in person than his pictures, if that was even possible.

"But we are together now," Calum smiled. He reached out to smooth one of Maddie's flyaway hairs. "What are your plans for when you are here? Where are you staying?"

"Well," Maddie said, a bit perplexed. "I didn't mean to be presumptuous, but I was hoping we could spend time together. I was thinking maybe I could stay with you."

"Oh," Calum said, looking surprised. "Sure, I mean you're definitely welcome to. My flat is pretty small, but I can work with tight spaces if you know what I mean."

Maddie really had no idea what exactly he was trying to say unless he was attempting to get at something crass, so she laughed nervously and took a sip of the beer. Nick walked up to the booth and slammed Calum's drink down, turning around and storming back behind the bar.

He picked up his glass and clinked it against Maddie's beer. "To our time together," Calum said.

"To us," Maddie said, smiling as she cheered their budding relationship.

Talking to Calum was not as nerve-wracking as Maddie worried it was going to be. She rarely had trouble talking to people about anything, but was worried that she would make a fool out of herself in front of Calum. However, she did not feel uncomfortable at all, other than wanting to look good for him. She found herself fussing over her clothes more than she usually did, making sure everything was in order.

Calum smiled at her as he sipped his drink. His skin was perfect, his hair was pristine, and his outfit looked like somebody professionally styled him. He was walking, talking Photoshop.

"I'm so excited to be here!" Maddie said, leaning in closer to Calum.

"I'm so happy you're here," Calum said, reaching out to rub Maddie's back gently. Maddie could smell his cologne. It was a peppery, dark scent that she just knew smelled expensive but after inhaling too much of it, she held back a sneeze. She sighed contentedly as she snuggled up closer to him in the booth.

"Oh!" Maddie said, pulling out her phone. "We should take a picture together!"

"Sure," Calum said, pulling away to straighten out his hair as he looked on the back-facing camera of his phone.

Maddie laughed as they leaned closer together and snapped a few selfies. She tucked the phone back into her pocket. Looking over, she saw Calum on his phone, furiously typing out messages. He seemed to sense her gaze, and looked up at her. He quickly tucked the phone in his pocket, then downed the rest of his drink.

"You ready to get out of here?" Calum asked, reaching for her hand.

"Yes!" Maddie replied, eager for whatever came next. They stood up from the booth. Calum threw some cash on the table and reached for Maddie's hand.

"I just have to go get my things," Maddie explained. "I stayed upstairs last night," she said.

"With O'Shaughnessy?" Calum asked, practically sneering as he said his name.

"No, in a different flat," Maddie said, shaking her head. She didn't understand what Calum's issue was.

Nick did her a favor, and she considered him a friend. Calum should be grateful that he helped her.

Maddie smiled at Nick as she walked up to the bar. Nick looked up from a book he was reading and glanced at Maddie. His eyes grew wide as he saw her standing with Calum.

"I just need to get upstairs to get my things," Maddie said. "Okay to come around back?"

"Sure," Nick said, reaching for the swinging door to let her behind the bar.

"Thanks," she said, striding behind the bar to the back door. As she climbed the stairs, Maddie's heart beat fast in anticipation. Her Prince Charming was here, in the flesh.

Maddie quickly gathered her things and zipped her suitcase shut. As she was zipping it, she spotted her copy of *Captivated by the Highland Laird* on top of her clothes. Smiling, she rubbed her hand over the cover before closing up the suitcase.

She could hear someone coming up the stairs outside as she locked up the apartment, reminding herself that she needed to give Nick the key back.

As she turned around in the hallway, Nick was at the top of the stairs, watching Maddie. His eyes looked sad as he watched her, waiting to see what she was going to say.

"I'll take your bag for you," Nick said. "It can be hard to get it down these bloody old stairs."

"Thanks, Nick," Maddie said, smiling. "I really appreciate everything you've done for me," she said, walking towards him with her bag.

Nick picked up the bag effortlessly and walked towards the stairs. "Maddie?" Nick asked, turning around at the top of the landing. She could smell his gentle scent of soap and something familiar. Was it pine? Freshly cut wood? Whatever it was, it was comforting.

"Yeah?" she replied, her eyes searching his face.

"Please remember what I said about Calum," he said, urging her to *hear* him.

"I know Calum used to be a playboy, but things are different with us," Maddie said, shaking her head. "You'll see," she continued, reaching out to rub his arm.

With a grunt, he carried her suitcase downstairs. Calum was watching the game on the television as a young teenager wiped down the bar. "Thanks for watching it, Jimmy," Nick said, nodding to the boy.

Maddie reached out to hand Nick the key, then jumped up and wrapped him in a big hug. "Thanks so much for everything, Nicholas" she said using his full name. Then, quietly, she whispered, "You're one of the good ones."

After promising to come visit him before she left Scotland, Maddie pulled her suitcase along the old wooden floor of the bar. Calum held out his hand and Maddie spun the suitcase to give it to him to manage. The confused look on his face made her realize that he wanted her hand, not the luggage, and she laughed as she switched the luggage around so she was wheeling it along and holding his hand.

As they walked out of the bar and got into an Uber, Maddie took one look back into the pub and saw Nick standing at the window, a towel tossed over his shoulder, watching her with a scowl on his face.

Chapter 4

The ride in the Uber was short as they drove through downtown Glasgow. It was a dark, dreary day. The wind was picking up, and Maddie smoothed out her hair as she took in the sights. The old buildings fascinated her.

Before long, they pulled up to a brand new apartment complex. It was modern and looked quite expensive. They stepped outside and Maddie wheeled her suitcase up on the sidewalk, letting the cold air hit her face. She was in a state of overheat around Calum. Maddie still couldn't believe she was here with him. After so many long nights spent talking to him, she was finally next to him, ready for whatever he wanted to do to win her heart.

They took the elevator up to his flat and Maddie smiled as he reached out to catch her hand. Once inside, Maddie was shocked at how small it really was. While everything was clean and contemporary, the room was extremely small. A tiny bed was in the corner of the studio apartment. Racks and racks of clothes took up the rest of the flat. Maddie's eyes grew wide as she took in the clothes, hardly believing that they could belong to one man.

There was no seating except for the bed. She sat down gently on the bed, looking around. A large TV practically covered one of the walls. Calum walked into the kitchenette and poured himself a glass of water, then downed it.

After gulping down the water, he turned toward Maddie. "Can I get you anything?" he asked, smiling at her.

"I'm fine for now, thanks," she said, smiling in return. Calum was definitely a bachelor. Anybody would be able to tell that just from looking at his flat. She was happy that at least the bed was cozy, and blushed as she thought about spending time in it.

Calum smiled at her as he strode over, taking off his jacket to reveal a tight white t-shirt. Maddie could see his slight abs underneath the shirt, and nearly drooled as she looked at his lithe, toned body.

Calum sat next to her on the bed, a hand beginning to rub her thigh. Maddie's heart was practically beating out of her chest with every touch from Calum.

"Come here," he murmured, grabbing her shoulder as he leaned closer. His smooth hands enveloped her face, drawing her nearer to his own.

Slowly, but forcefully, he began to kiss her. Maddie's heart was beating faster and she began heating up as the kiss continued.

She allowed him to slide his tongue between her lips, enjoying the new experience. His soft lips pressed on, furthering the kiss. Before she knew it, he was laying back on the bed and pulling Maddie with him.

As she leaned over him, they continued to make out, with Calum's hands roaming up and down her body. Calum broke the kiss momentarily to grab her arm, dragging it slowly down towards his erection. Maddie's eyes grew wide as she felt it through his skinny jeans, not exactly knowing what he expected her to do. She rubbed it slowly, pretending as if she knew what men liked.

Calum moaned as he grasped her breasts. Quickly, he broke the kiss and grabbed her hips, flipping her over so that he was on top of her. As he flipped her, however, Maddie smacked her head on the wall. "Shit!" she shouted as she grabbed her head.

"Oh no!" Calum said, stifling a giggle. "Are you okay?" Maddie held back tears as the pain made her head throb. She had a hard knock to the head, and was discombobulated for a moment.

She pushed Calum off of her as she sat up, wincing in pain. "Do you have ice?" Maddie asked, hoping that applying cold might help.

"Calum jumped up from the bed and strode to his small refrigerator. Pulling a package of frozen edamame out, he brought it over to her and Maddie placed it on the spot.

"You'll be okay," Calum said. "It was just a bump."

Maddie ignored him as she held the bag on her head, shaking her head gently.

After sitting for a few minutes trying to get her bearings, Calum pulled out his phone. The two sat in silence and Maddie laid back down on the bed, feeling much better. She tossed the edamame onto the nightstand as she put her head down.

"So sorry I interrupted our fun time," she said, looking over to Calum on the end of the bed.

Calum smiled and tucked his phone in his pocket. "There's plenty of time for that," he said, coming over to lay down next to her. "Why don't you nap a bit, and then we can go out and I'll show you Glasgow at night?"

"I'd adore that!" Maddie exclaimed, excited for what the night held.

Calum kissed Maddie's temple then slid down next to her, his arm draping around her hips. The bed was small, but since they were both trim people, there was plenty of room.

Maddie quickly found sleep as she listened to Calum's quiet breathing. She managed to doze for a bit before she was awakened from the sound of tapping. She peeked one eye open to see Calum sitting next to her, typing a message on his phone with his thumbs. He had a smile on his face.

"Hey," she said. "How long did I sleep for?" she asked, stifling a yawn.

"About two hours," Calum said, reluctantly tearing his eyes from the phone. "Want to get ready to go out?"

"Sure," Maddie said, excitedly. "Do you have a coffeemaker?"

"No," Calum said, his voice strong. "I never drink the stuff. Terrible for the teeth," he explained, then opened his mouth to show his perfectly whitened teeth.

"Gotcha," Maddie said, looking away and trying to keep her own mouth shut as much as possible while she spoke.

"I'm going to get ready and then you can, okay?" he asked.

"That sounds fine," Maddie said, smiling up at Calum as he walked to the bathroom. The door shut with a click and she heard the shower turn on moments later. Maddie stood up to grab her phone from her jacket pocket, then laid back on the bed.

She flipped through the photos of her and Calum at the pub. She picked one that she liked best and sent it to her sister and their good friend, Shannon, in an email. "Having the best time ever," Maddie wrote. "I met this amazing man and had to come over to see him in person," she continued. After sending the email, Maddie put her head back on the pillow and scanned through the photos again. She opened up Instagram and posted the photo, tagging Calum.

Two minutes later, her phone began to ring with a video chat request from Melissa. Sitting up in the bed, Maddie accepted the call. Once it loaded, she saw Melissa, Shannon, and Jakob all staring into the phone, a look of concern on each of their faces.

"Madeline Rebecca Danzer!" Melissa scolded, her brows furrowed in concern. "What the hell are you doing?"

Smiling, Maddie relaxed. "I'm fine," she pleaded. "Calum and I met on Instagram and we've been talking for weeks now. I decided that we needed to meet so I flew here. I'm having the best time!" she insisted, trying to convince them that everything was fine.

"We don't know anything about this guy," Melissa said, knowing that caution was best when it came to meeting men on the Internet.

"Seriously, Maddie, we are so worried about you," Shannon said, concern in her voice as she nervously twisted her nose ring. "What is this guy's name?" she asked.

"Calum MacGregor," Maddie said quietly. "He's a model. He's on the cover of romance novels and things like that," Maddie said. She explained how they met and how they had been talking for weeks. She talked about how hospitable everyone had been to her in Scotland, thinking of Nick.

"Interesting," Melissa said, her voice full of concern. "I didn't know you were into the model type," she continued.

"Speak for yourself, sis!" Maddie replied, her eyes growing wide as she looked at Melissa's own dreamboat. Jakob laughed and began to blush furiously. Melissa smiled as she gazed over at him. Shannon merely sighed.

"Promise me you'll be careful?" Shannon asked, a pleading tone in her voice.

"I promise," Maddie said. "Believe me, you guys, he's the real deal! I am sorry I didn't tell you sooner," she said quietly. "I will send you more pictures of us right after I get off the phone."

"Call one of us every day. Or at the very least email us, okay?" Melissa asked. "No excuses."

"I promise," Maddie said with a smile. She already missed her sister, and even Jakob too. She missed Shannon's protective nature.

After saying goodbye, Maddie sent another version of the selfie they took in the bar and another outside O'Shaughnessy's. Maddie looked towards the bathroom. Calum was still in there getting ready. How long did it possibly take to throw on some new clothes?

She walked around his tiny flat, then looked at his extensive wardrobe. The labels were all designer, and she had no doubt that the rack of clothes probably cost more than everything she owned.

Maddie was rubbing the leather accents on a vest when the bathroom door opened. Calum strode out of the bathroom like he was on a catwalk. He was wearing a pair of red skinny jeans and a worn black v-neck shirt. His blonde hair was artfully gelled, and if Maddie wasn't mistaken, he had a bit of eyeliner on.

With wide eyes, Maddie took in his outfit. Calum walked over to her, smacked her butt, and said, "Don't be too long, okay? We have places to be." Her eyes narrowed as he said that, and instead of picking a fight, Maddie silently walked into the bathroom, grabbing her bag of toiletries as she went.

After touching up her makeup and teasing her hair, Maddie slid on a mustard yellow sweater dress and paired it with tights and some heeled boots. Feeling satisfied with her outfit, she came out of the bathroom. Calum was in his kitchenette, leaning up against the counter and tapping his foot as he glanced at his phone.

"Ready?" Calum asked, pushing himself up from the counter and walking over to Maddie. He pulled Maddie into his arms, then leaned down to kiss her.

Maddie sighed contentedly after the kiss, still shocked that she was here with this man. Hand in hand, the two walked down the stairs to the sidewalk, an Uber waiting for them.

"So where are we going to dinner?" Maddie asked as she slid into the backseat and Calum followed suit.

"A nice little steakhouse downtown," Calum said.

"Do you think I'm dressed okay?" Maddie asked, now self-conscious about her outfit.

"Yes, it's perfect," Calum said, smiling at her as he pulled out his phone. He set his hand on Maddie's thigh as he used his other hand to reply to a text message, the phone pointed away from Maddie.

"Who are you talking to?" Maddie asked, desperate to make conversation.

"Hmm?" Calum said a moment later. "Oh, no one," he said, sliding the phone into his pocket and smiling at Maddie. She couldn't hide her frown as she watched his movements. Was he texting other women? Or, just maybe, was he planning a surprise for her? Before she could berate her imagination for sounding naive, Maddie decided to forget common sense for just a moment and to treasure the thought.

Smiling, she smoothed the hem of her dress and looked out the window, taking in Glasgow in the evening. It was a beautiful city, she mused, and she could hardly wait to explore it more.

They walked into Bryant's and Maddie immediately knew this restaurant was out of her league. With crisp white tablecloths and modern decor, the restaurant was contemporary and hip. Its clientele were impeccably dressed and probably some of the classiest people that Maddie had ever seen.

As the hostess gushed at Calum and gave him a hug, Maddie looked down at her outfit and felt incredibly frumpy. Clearing her throat and holding her head up high, she linked her arm around Calum's and walked into the restaurant behind the hostess, who frequently did a double-take to smile at Calum.

Calum ordered a bottle of wine for the table, and Maddie sipped on it as she got comfortable.

"So tell me more about you," Maddie said. "I want to know everything," she smiled.

"Everything, eh?" Calum replied, a glimmer of laughter in his eyes. "Not much to know about me, I suppose. I'm living the dream," he said, un-ironically.

"I see," Maddie said. "What about your childhood?"

"The usual, I suppose. Just Mum and Dad, no brothers or sisters," he said.

"Are you close to them?" Maddie asked.

"I suppose. I see them on holidays unless I am out of town on a shoot. What about you?" Calum asked.

"Oh, I thought I told you. I am only close to my sister. Both of my parents are dead," Maddie explained, holding up her wine glass to take another sip. Maddie was prepared to tell people the basic facts about her life, but telling Calum her entire family history? That would have to wait. It wasn't every day you had to tell the man you hoped to date that your father killed your mother, and today was *not* that day.

The waiter came to take their order. Maddie ordered a steak and shrimp. Calum ordered a salad. Maddie's eyes grew wide after the waiter left. She leaned forward and said, "Calum, you know we are at a steakhouse, right?"

"Swimsuit shoot this week," he explained. "I have to be trim. By the way, how do you feel about coming to the gym with me tomorrow morning? We could both use some toning, and you'll need it after that steak."

With a loud gasp, Maddie sat back in her chair and stared at Calum. She had never expected to hear something so outrageous and uncalled for from her date.

"Let's get one thing straight here, Calum," Maddie explained, absentmindedly grasping her steak knife. "Asking me to accompany you to the gym is one thing. That's fine, I get it. But if you ever attempt to body shame me again, we are going to have a serious problem, okay?"

"I'm sorry you took it that way!" Calum explained. "It certainly was not my intention at all."

Tilting her head to the side, Maddie moved on from gripping the knife to fiddling with a piece of her hair that always curled. "I see," she explained. "Like I said, it can't happen again."

"Got it," Calum said, downing a glass of water.

After a particularly droll meal, with Maddie stuffing the steak and shrimp into her mouth and watching Calum munch on his salad, he paid the bill and they were on their way.

Maddie had just enough wine in her system to allow herself to have a good time and as they made their way to the nightclub, she was ready to dance.

They waited no more than two minutes in line before she and Calum were admitted. After checking her jacket, Maddie got a drink from the bar while Calum opted for water. The club music was blaring as people around them laughed and had a good time. It was dark in the club save for the neon lights illuminating the room. They made their way to the dance floor and began to dance. Calum and Maddie were grinding on the dance floor to the loud electronic music. Sweaty bodies crowded around them.

No matter how much she tried, she just could not find a good rhythm with Calum. She felt awkward and clumsy, and Maddie *never* felt that way while dancing. After Maddie finished her drink and set it on a nearby table, Calum grabbed her hand and pulled her to the hallway with the bathrooms. Rounding the corner, he pushed Maddie up against the wall and began making out with her, pressing his body into hers.

The alcohol mixed with the distant bass of the music , making Maddie's head ache. She allowed Calum to kiss her neck, having his way with her. Realizing that she was not into it, Maddie thought she must be tired. Gently pushing him away, she said, "I'm really tired. Can we go to bed?"

"It's not even ten," Calum whined, looking at her as if she was crazy.

"I know," Maddie said, "But I'm not feeling great at all," she explained.

"I'm not ready to go home yet," Calum said. Digging his hand into the pocket of his jeans, he fished out his apartment key. "You can take an Uber home. I'll be back later."

She stared at outstretched hand with the key and scoffed. She grabbed the key and left to get her jacket, not bothering to look back at him.

Maddie stood outside the club, trying diligently to clear her head and looked at her phone to bring up Calum's address, which she had typed in earlier that day in case she needed it. As she waited for an Uber, she took a deep breath and exhaled into the cold of the night.

Looking around, she smiled at the groups of friends having a fun night out. She missed her sister and Shannon, and wished she was having a fun girls night instead of this. This was not how things were supposed to go at all.

Rain began to pour once she was in the car, the lights of the city becoming blurry through the raindrops on the window. Calum's ridiculous behavior was so uncalled for. He left her alone in a foreign country at a nightclub when she didn't feel good. What kind of man did that? Not her hero.

Once she was inside Calum's flat, Maddie told herself she would just lay down for an hour or two before figuring out what to do. Her head throbbed and she only bothered to toss her jacket and boots off before falling into his bed, not even allowing feelings of self-pity to form before falling asleep.

Chapter 5

The only explanation for what happened next was that Maddie was trapped in a bad dream. She was dead to the world when she heard a crash and then someone began groping her. She awoke to a very drunk, very disgusting Calum on top of her, grabbing her breasts and attempting to kiss her.

Maddie pushed him off of her and jumped out of the bed, pulling her glasses off the bedside table and slipping them on. "What the actual fuck?" she shouted. "What do you think you're doing?"

"Calm down," Calum hissed. "You're such a prude, Lisa."

"Lisa?" Maddie exclaimed. "Who is Lisa?"

"Maddie. Maddie," Calum repeated. "If you're going to leave me at the club, the least you can do is put out," he slurred.

"Is this a damn joke?" she shouted, turning the light beside the bed on. "I came all the way from the States to see you," Maddie said. "The least you could do is treat me with some respect," she said, crossing her arms in front of her as she took in the sorry sight of Calum sitting on his bed.

"Why are you here anyway?" he asked.

"What do you mean?" Maddie implored. "We were talking for weeks. We had something. I had to meet you in person."

"It was just flirting," Calum slurred, standing up to face her. "And then next thing I know you're on my doorstep. You're a nice enough bird but not my type at all," he explained. "I mean, I'd fuck you but that's about it."

Maddie's cheeks heated as she listened to Calum talk. She couldn't be in this apartment any longer. Rushing to the bathroom, she gathered her makeup bag and threw it into her suitcase. *Don't cry don't cry don't cry* she told herself over and over.

Maddie zipped up the suitcase and hauled it onto its wheels. Taking one last look at Calum, whose phone was chiming with what appeared to be Tinder notifications, Maddie scoffed and left the apartment. She stood in the hallway for longer than she was willing to admit, just trying to figure out a plan.

She had never been so ashamed in her entire life. This trip was supposed to be everything for her. It was supposed to be her future. She really thought she had found the one with Calum. The way she was captivated with him the moment she set eyes on him was indicative enough, no?

Maddie had never been so enamored with someone in all of her life, and she was so sure that life would work out for her this time. Now she was embarrassed and disgusted. She wanted nothing else than to crawl into her bed at home and forget about everything, but she had to figure something out before she could show her face back home. She just spent a gross amount of time reassuring Melissa and Shannon that she was in it to win it with Calum and here she was, a giant fool.

Walking out of the building and onto the sidewalk, Maddie discovered that the rain had picked up. It was cold and wet outside and she was angry that she had to spend her money on a hotel, yet they were undoubtedly still all booked anyway. Before she could change her mind, Maddie called for an Uber and waited for it impatiently, knowing that she really only had one place to go for advice.

The door to O'Shaughnessy's was still open when Maddie arrived around midnight, soaked and emotionally exhausted. As she hauled her suitcase into the bar once more, she could have laughed as she thought about how this is exactly how she started her Scotland journey, so full of hope.

The bar was dark, as always, and she spotted two old men shooting pool and insulting each others' game. They looked up at her, nodded, then went back to playing. Aside from Nick, who was standing in the kitchen at the grill, intent on his work, the bar was empty. She rolled her suitcase up to the bar and took off her soaking wet jacket.

Nick looked up through the kitchen window as she stood in front of him. He looked shocked as he saw the sad look on her face. Nick came rushing out from the kitchen, still wearing the white apron. He ran around the bar and took in Maddie. Her hair was soaked, her dress was stretched out every which way, and she was pretty certain her eyeliner was running down her face.

"What happened, love?" he asked. Before he knew it, Maddie was running into his arms, enveloped in his strong body. Her body began shaking as she started to cry, angry with herself for being emotional.

"Fookin' 'ell, I'll pummel him," Nick murmured as he wrapped his arms tighter around Maddie. After she calmed down, Nick released Maddie to get her a glass of water, leading her to a barstool so that she could sit down.

"Tell me everything," he said as he sat down next to her.

Maddie took a deep breath, then sipped the water before she delved into the story of her disaster night, not leaving one detail out. As she relayed her story, Nick murmured curse words under his breath, his accent so strong that she couldn't make all of them out

"I feel like such a fool," Maddie said. "I should have listened to you when you told me about Calum, but I was so stupid and thought maybe it was real," she said. "I miss home but I can't go back before I figure out a way to explain this to my sister," she furthered.

"You are from Wisconsin, right?" Nick asked gruffly next to her, not taking his eyes off of her.

"Yes, why?" Maddie asked, ending her question with a hiccup. Not saying a word, Nick went into the kitchen, busying himself with making something. Maddie watched as he focused on the task at hand, his brow furrowed as he concentrated on what he was making.

A few minutes later, he brought her out a plate and set it in front of her.

"Grilled cheese?" she laughed as she saw what he had made for her. "That's so sweet," she said.

"Well, I figured that since you waxed poetic about cheese *and* you live in Wisconsin that you like cheese," he said quietly, "and you must be hungry."

"Ugh, I don't think I can eat right now," Maddie said, grabbing her stomach. Nick looked at her with a shocked expression and she laughed. "You're right," she said. "I can always eat."

He smiled as she lifted the sandwich to her lips, the butter practically dripping onto the plate. After taking one bite, then another, Maddie savored the flavors as she munched on the sandwich.

"Good?" Nick asked, a smile on his face.

"This is the best grilled cheese I've ever had," Maddie exclaimed. "It's even better than at the state fair and that's saying a lot," she furthered.

"I'm glad you like it, Maddie," Nick said, leaning up against the bar as he watched her eat. He was absolutely captivated with her, and she didn't even realize it.

"Has it been busy tonight?" Maddie asked hopefully. Nick's blue eyes looked around the bar and Maddie followed suit, eyeing the two men who were putting their jackets on to leave.

"It's been about this busy," Nick deadpanned, going to lock up after the men. He started his nightly routine, flipping the chairs up on the tables and turning off lights. Maddie took her empty plate into the kitchen of the bar. Seeing a stack of dishes to be done, she turned on the hot water, got out soap, and began to wash them.

Carefully, she scrubbed the dishes with a sponge and rinsed them clean, setting them on a drying rack. She was focused on intently cleaning a fry pan, scrubbing the years of char on it while sweat began to cover her brow, when the deep sound of a throat clearing behind her made her jump.

Hands still in the sink, Maddie craned her neck around to see Nick standing behind her, his hands on his trim hips. "What the ever-loving fook do you think you're doing?" he asked her sternly.

With a clatter, Maddie dropped the pan and turned around, wiping her hands on her sweater dress.

"I'm sorry," Maddie said, shocked at his outburst. "I clean when I'm stressed."

Dropping his hands to his sides, Nick took a step back. "No, Maddie," he said, quieter now, "Don't apologize. You've had a long night. I didn't want you to think you had to work. Leave the dishes, please, and get some rest."

Biting her bottom lip, Maddie pondered his request. "Can I just finish this pan?" she asked him, a glimmer of humor in her eyes.

With a low, deep laugh, Nick said, "Sure, love, finish the pan." Spinning around, she hurriedly scrubbed the pan and rinsed it, setting it on the drying tray with the rest of the dishes. She wiped up the water on the counter and immediately felt relief, even though she was still nervous about the future.

Nick came back into the kitchen, this time with her suitcase in hand. It occurred to her that she never even asked if she could stay. "Oh," Maddie began. "Please don't think I just expected to stay here. I was going to ask you about hotels. I am not going to be doing as much sightseeing as I thought, and I can afford one. If you could just recommend one to me, I will be out of your hair."

Nick stood in front of her, standing her suitcase up and then extending to his full height.

"Did you sleep well last night?" Nick asked. "Did you get the rest you needed here?"

Eyes wide, Maddie pondered it. "Yes, it was the best sleep of my life," she said honestly.

"Then here you'll stay," Nick said firmly, dragging her suitcase to the staircase and starting up the stairs.

After he was halfway up the stairs, hauling her suitcase with him, he turned around and looked at Maddie, who was still standing in the middle of the darkened kitchen, watching him go. "Are you coming?" he asked.

"Yes, of course," Maddie said hurriedly, quickly snapping out of whatever trance she was in. Bouncing up the stairs, she made it onto the landing where Nick already had the door to the flat unlocked, and her suitcase placed inside it once more.

She stepped inside. It was just as she had left it earlier that morning. She kneeled down to unzip her boots, which were still soaked from the rain. Being careful to not get them on the hardwood floor, she propped them onto a rug and peeled her socks off, going barefoot.

"You just rest for as long as you need to," Nick said. "I mean it."

"Thanks Nick," Maddie said, shivering a bit now that she was barefoot, just glad to have such a generous and kind person in front of her.

"Anytime," Nick said, walking to the thermostat to fiddle with the temperature. Almost immediately, hot air began pumping through the vents. "You should warm up soon, love," he said, walking to the door.

"Thanks again, Nicholas," Maddie reiterated, walking to the door to lock up behind him. With a nod, he walked out and gently closed the door behind her with a click.

After turning the locks, Maddie swung around and pressed her back against the door, exhaling out an enormous sigh. It seemed to her that there were many things that were not what they appeared, including her romance with Calum.

Walking to the bathroom, Maddie gently took off her clothes and set them in a pile on the floor. She reached into the shower to turn it on, hot steam emanating out just moments later.

With a sigh of relief, she stepped into the shower, letting the hot water pour down upon her. She stood there for what must have been minutes, willing the tension to fall out of her body. Maddie hated rejection, but she was used to being alone. Of course it stung that Calum turned out to be a dolt, but at least she found out the real him before it was too late.

After shampooing her hair and cleansing her body with a soft loofah, she stepped out of the shower and wrapped her body in an oversized pink plush towel. The softness of the towel enveloped her and kept her warm as she walked to the bed, phone in hand.

She opened up her email app, and began typing a message to Melissa.

"Sis," she began. "Where to begin? Scotland is amazing. The buildings are so beautiful. I know you would be itching to photograph them all. I am having the best time here. Things are going so well. I have a good feeling about this. How is Jakob? Did you pick a date for the wedding yet? Off to bed, but I will talk to you soon! Love you." Before she could change her mind, Maddie pressed "send" and set her phone on the nightstand.

Too tired to change, Maddie let the towel drop to the floor and crawled naked under the covers, sleep taking over her before she even had a chance to reflect on her day.

Hours later, Maddie woke with a start. Sitting up in the bed, she looked around and realized it was still dark outside, not nearly time to wake up. Walking to the kitchen, she found a cup in the cabinet and poured herself a glass of water. Standing naked in the kitchen, she drank the entire glass and then went back to the bedroom, sprawling out in the bed.

Her phone lit up on the nightstand. Maddie grabbed it and realized it was her sister emailing her back. "Mads," her sister wrote, "I am glad you are having a nice time. Send some pictures! Is Calum treating you well? What are you doing for fun? I love you!"

Deciding to wait until the morning to reply, she settled back into bed and fell back asleep, knowing she needed a few more hours of rest.

The sound of cars speeding past woke Maddie up, sun now streaming from the windows. With a loud yawn, she sat up in bed and looked at the clock. It was 8:30 in the morning. Padding over to the kitchen, she found the coffeemaker and brewed a cup, inhaling the deep aroma of the coffee.

After unzipping her suitcase, she threw on a pair of jeans and a light pink sweater, a pair of moccasins on her feet. She quickly emailed her sister back with some pictures of the city lights and one that Maddie snapped of the outside of the bar when she first arrived. "Of course he is treating me well," Maddie lied. "Sightseeing today! Can't wait to send pictures." Maddie felt terrible about lying to her sister, but was not ready to tell her the truth. After sipping the coffee, she walked out of the flat, locking it behind her.

She tiptoed down the creaky steps, wondering what Nick was doing. Was he still in his flat? Or perhaps working downstairs working on something at the bar?

She found the bar completely empty, all of the lights still shut off. Sunlight streamed through the stained glass window on the door of the pub, and it guided her eye to the back door off of the kitchen. Pushing open the door, Maddie found a small space of grass and a large shed behind the building. Walking down the path toward the shed, she could hear a repetitive scraping sound.

She walked up to the closed door and peered through the window. Her eyes grew wide as she took in Nick standing in the middle of the pine-paneled shop, his entire body moving with force as he took a hand planer to a piece of wood. Maddie watched intently, fascinated with his craft.

He was surrounded by boards of all shapes and sizes. Wood was everywhere. Large machines were aligned against the walls, dozens of hand tools displayed on a peg board.

Before she could stop it, the door creaked open in front of her. Nick stopped his movements, startled at the noise. He looked up at Maddie, setting the planer down. Maddie stepped carefully into the shop, sensing that this was Nick's sacred space.

"Hi," she said sheepishly, eyes fascinated with all of the tools. She had never seen anything like it.

"Good morning," Nick said quietly, wiping the sweat on his brow with the back of his hand. He stepped away from the workbench to come out towards her.

"I didn't mean to disturb you," she said nervously. "I was just exploring and saw the shed."

"Don't worry about it, Maddie," Nick said, a bit roughly. "This is my shop."

"Wow," Maddie said as she looked around once more. Dozens of beautifully handcrafted items were scattered about the room, from delicate wood-turned bowls to tables and chests. The detail was meticulous, every angle and curve so very clearly carefully thought out. "You did all this?" she asked incredulously.

"It's nothing, just a hobby," Nick said, the blush rising above his light brown beard.

"It's more than a hobby," Maddie said, her small fingertips tracing smooth top of a side table. "It's beautiful work, Nick. You are incredibly talented."

"I don't know about all that," he said. "Just a way to make some money on the side." His accent grew heavier as he followed Maddie throughout the shop, stopping every few feet to look at something else.

"You could do this full time," she said. "I'm surprised you don't."

"Well, I've got the pub..." he said. Maddie nodded, remembering just how bare it was the two nights she was there. He couldn't possibly be making a profit with the small amount of customers. Why did he keep it going? Because it was his family's? Shaking the questions from her head, Maddie allowed Nick to show her how the wood lathe that she was standing in front of worked to allow chunks of wood to be carved into bowls and other decorative ornaments.

She was amazed at how fast the machine spun around, and when Nick handed her a pair of safety glasses, her adventurous spirit soared.

Carefully placing them over her own pair of black frames, she watched as he used a long carving tool to sculpt the wood Thin strips of wood flew to the ground around them, his large arm carefully holding the tool.

Before she knew it, the block of wood began to resemble a small bowl. Maddie realized that she had been holding her breath throughout the process, and quickly exhaled just as Nick set the tool down and powered off the machine.

"With some sanding and a few coats of polyurethane, it will be a bowl in no time," Nick said, smiling wryly over at her.

"That's so wonderful, Nick," Maddie said, ecstatic about her miniature field trip.

"I don't know about wonderful," Nick laughed.

"It is!" Maddie insisted, following him as he brushed the wood chips off of his flannel shirt and walked to the door.

"That's kind of you, Maddie," Nick said quietly. As they walked back towards the pub, he asked, "Have you eaten anything?" As if on cue, Maddie felt her stomach grumble and she shook her head.

She followed him through the bar and onto the busy sidewalk. They stepped into the cafe next door. The invigorating smell of coffee and espresso wafted to Maddie and she inhaled enjoyably.

The small cafe was cute, and plenty of people were spread about working on their laptops or reading the newspaper. As they walked up to the counter, Maddie realized that she recognized the redhead taking orders as the girl who was in the pub the day before laughing with Nick.

The girl broke out into a wide smile as she saw Nick. "Hello Mr. O'Shaughnessy. What can I get you today?"

"Just fine, Mrs. O'Shaughnessy," he smiled. Maddie nearly fell over as he said the words. Nick was married? She never would have guessed it! Taking a step back, Maddie tried to swallow her shock as she followed through with her own order of black coffee and a muffin, insisting on paying for both of their coffees. It was the least she could do for his kindness.

Nick grabbed their coffees, winking at the redhead before he swirled around and motioned to a free table. Wouldn't that be just a bit awkward, to sit and chitchat with a married man while his wife worked away? "I think I'll just take my coffee back to the flat," Maddie said. "You should keep your wife company," she said.

"Me what now? Me wife?" Nick nearly shouted. Maddie couldn't help but notice that his accent got even stronger when he was shocked or upset. "That's my cousin Lyle's wife!" He said, a smile erupting across his face.

"Oh," Maddie said, relieved that she was out of that awkward situation. She would rather be laughed at than be trapped in awkwardness. "Haha, I guess there are lots of O'Shaughnessys around here," Maddie said with a laugh. "That's my bad."

With a deep laugh, Nick pulled out a chair and sat down. Maddie took a seat across from him, still holding onto her muffin.

"So you're not married, right?" Maddie asked with a smile.

"Definitely not," Nick said, then let out a deep breath.

"I'm glad we got that cleared up," Maddie said with a wink.

"As am I," Nick said as he took a sip of his coffee, stray wood chips still clinging to his flannel.

Out of instinct, Maddie reached to pick them off of his shirt, then thought the better of it. Instead, she nodded to his shirt, and he pulled off the wood chips. Better to play it safe, she thought. Safe was best.

Chapter 6

As they walked back to the bar, Maddie took a deep breath of the cool morning air. There was no snow on the ground, but she sensed that it could snow at any second. The crisp air hit her face with a gust of wind and made her wake up from her daze.

"Have you ever been to the public library here?" Maddie asked him. "Since I'm a librarian back home and wanted to check it out while I am here."

"Of course," Nick said matter-of-factly. "I go to the Mitchell weekly. I'll take you," he said assuredly.

"Really?" Maddie asked, filling with glee. "I'd love that!" she said. She could have sworn that, beneath his gruff demeanor and that thick beard, he was grinning a bit.

"Are you shocked that I will take you or that I use my public library?" Nick asked, looking down at her as he held the door of the bar open for her.

"Uhhh," Maddie replied. "Well, I have been working in libraries for a while now and you don't look like any patron I've ever seen."

"Oh really?" Nick replied playfully. "Give it a few years and I'll be fully gray soon enough."

"Very funny," Maddie said. "How old are you anyway?"

Nick grunted as he went behind the bar and to some keys hanging up on the wall. He plucked a key from the bunch and turned around. "Too old," he replied.

"Come on, Nicholas, you can tell me," she cooed.

"Thirty-seven," he replied. "You?"

"I'm twenty-six," Maddie replied matter-of-factly. "Thirty-seven is not old, mister. Cool your jets."

"Shite," Nick muttered under his breath. Then, turning to the door, he began striding out. "Come on, Maddie, we have a library to visit."

Maddie smiled as she jumped off the bar stool and ran after him, practically captivated by this mysterious, and apparently well-read, man.

When she got outside, Nick locked up the bar behind her and they walked to a dark blue pickup truck parked in front of the bar. Nick opened the door for her and motioned for Maddie to get in. She obliged, jumping up to get in the high vehicle.

Once Nick shut the door, her heart started to beat. She was excited for this adventure. Exploring new places—especially places with books—was her favorite thing to do.

Nick got in the truck next to her. She could smell the scent of fresh-cut pine on him, along with his soap. It was a pleasant scent, she mused, gentle but familiar.

As he began driving, Maddie decided to find out as much about him as possible.

"Where did you grow up?" she asked.

"A wee house right outside of Glasgow," Nick explained as he merged into traffic.

"Do you have any other siblings besides your sister?"

After a moment, Nick replied. "No. Just my wee sister, Rosie. It's hard to believe she's getting married in less than a week," he said, shaking his head.

"How old is she?" Maddie asked. The way Nick spoke about her, she was expecting her to be a child bride.

"Thirty-five," Nick said. Maddie tried to stifle a giggle at that. He was incredibly protective of her, she could tell.

"And your parents?" Maddie asked.

"Mum and Dad still live in the house we grew up in. Mum is a nurse at the hospital. Dad is retired police," he explained. "Enough about me, what about your family?"

Maddie explained how her sister had met and fallen in love with Jakob and how it was just the two of them in her family. "Not to be super depressing," Maddie explained, "but my family situation was a little dysfunctional. To put it simply, my father was an abusive asshat and my mother is dead because of it." Maddie felt a sense of relief as she purged the information. She was a very open person, but not the type to readily tell people that information.

Nick took his eyes off the road to look at Maddie, his brow furrowed in worry. "Oh, Maddie," he said. "I'm so sorry."

"Thanks," Maddie said.

"He hurt you too?" Nick asked quietly.

"Yes," Maddie admitted. "But that chapter of my life is over now."

Nodding, Nick looked back towards the road. His big hands gripped the steering wheel with sheer force. Although he was a quiet man, he seemed like he wanted to say something, anything. Before long, they drove up in front of the Mitchell Library. After Maddie's extensive research, she recognized it right away.

The enormous tan brick library was one of the most gorgeous buildings she had ever seen. It was like no library she ever witnessed, even in Chicago. The bronze dome roof, now green with time, was a beacon for people throughout the city. Ornate sculptures decorated the building, down to a Greek statue made of bronze on top of the roof. The building seemed to go on and on, and Maddie could hardly wait to see the thousands of books inside the building. Her heart beat faster as she thought about running up and down the four floors filled with volumes.

"I'm not in Wisconsin anymore," Maddie said, mostly to herself, as Nick parked. They walked up to the building and Maddie stood and stared, taking it all in. If possible, it looked even larger than in the photographs. A large circular portion of the building boasted enormous pillars. The rooftop doubled as a balcony. Maddie couldn't imagine standing on the roof, looking down at the city.

With a sigh, they walked towards the door. Maddie grabbed Nick's arm and looped her own through it, squeezing it a bit. "I am so freaking excited, Nick!" she said quietly. Nick tensed up at her touch, then relaxed a bit and continued to walk.

"Did you know that Andrew Carnegie laid the first stone for this building?" Nick asked her as he reached out to open the door. "Wait, that was a silly question. I have a feeling you already knew that."

Maddie laughed. "I did indeed know that, but you keep telling me those facts and I might faint."

Nick beamed as they walked inside. Maddie was shocked at how contemporary things appeared to be on the inside of the library. She could have easily been back home in her own library. A bustling cafe served coffee, making her homesick for Shannon's cozy coffee shop.

Children ran around, excitedly showing their parents their literary finds. Maddie smiled as she took it all in. Although she hadn't seen it before, Maddie watched Nick pull a book out from underneath his arm and slip it into the return.

"What do you like to read?" Maddie asked as she wandered around the library, browsing the displays.

"Thrillers, mostly. Some classics. What about you?" Nick asked, watching her intently as she looked around.

"I like romance," Maddie said proudly.

"I should have guessed," he said. When she looked up, Nick winked at her.

"Oh?" Maddie said. "How so?"

"You're a romantic," Nick said. "It's very clear."

"Hmm," she replied. Deciding not to touch that comment, she said, "Give me a tour."

"As you wish," Nick said.

They strode around the first floor. Maddie was slightly disappointed that the library was so contemporary. She really expected more. They took an elevator to the third floor. As she stepped out of the elevator, Maddie was shocked at the change. How quickly things could differ! She was suddenly transformed into a library of the 1940s or 50s. Card catalogs surrounded the big open room. Locked glass cases displayed rare books and artifacts. Maddie was in an archivist's heaven.

"What do you do at the library?" Nick asked her as they strolled around, Maddie nosily opening random card catalog drawers.

"I'm the assistant director," she said proudly.

Nick's eyes grew wide. "That's amazing!" he exclaimed. "You should be very proud of yourself."

"It's just a small library," Maddie explained. "Willow Falls isn't that big of a town. It's not like Milwaukee or Glasgow," she explained.

"Don't do that," he scolded. Maddie's brow furrowed as she listened to him. "That is a large accomplishment and I have no doubt that you could run *this* library someday if you wanted to."

Maddie reached out and touched his bicep, squeezing it a bit. "That's so sweet, Nicholas," she said. "You're too nice to me." He grunted in reply, then walked towards an old wooden door. He gestured for Maddie to open it. She looked around to the librarians' desk, as if to check if she was breaking a rule. They were preoccupied, so she opened the door anyway.

With a gasp, Maddie nearly started crying as she walked into the reading room. Three floors below, dozens of people studied quietly at dark cherry tables, green-glassed bankers lamps decorating the tables. The two stood on a narrow balcony that circled the entire room. Behind them, hundreds of books perched on oak shelves. Maddie nearly squealed as she observed the staircases which could lead them down to the main level.

The room was bright. Looking up, Maddie realized that the room was lit entirely by natural lighting, the whole ceiling a skylight. Looking at Nick as if for permission, he nodded and Maddie began to walk around the landing. They came to a staircase and Maddie walked down to the second floor.

"It's like the Beast's library," Maddie whispered, which was not really a whisper at all.

Nick smiled as people looked up from their studies to stare at Maddie.

"Nick, I feel like you and I know each other well enough now for me to ask you what I am about to ask you." Nick stilled as they stood on the staircase, no idea what she was about to ask of him.

"Will you please go on the main level and take glamour shots of me walking down this staircase? It's very important to me," Maddie said seriously.

"Of course," Nick said, a grin forming on his face. She handed him her cell phone and Nick slid around her to pass her on the staircase, his large body rubbing against hers as grazed past her. Maddie stilled as he touched her, convinced that static electricity was causing her temporary paralysis.

Shaking the thought out of her mind, Maddie got ready to pose on the staircase, her silliness coming out with the shots. She alternated between kiss faces and sultry, serious looks, nearly straddling the railing.

Nick laughed loudly as she started this and cheered her on, saying, "work it, girl." Maddie didn't expect him to be so into it. She usually had Melissa take her pictures since she was a photographer. It was great to see gruff and crabby Nick having so much fun. Maddie laughed as she walked down the stairs, reaching out for her phone.

Nick pulled the phone away out of her reach. "Wait a minute, Maddie," Nick said. "If I give you this phone back, you have to promise to send me these photographs."

Maddie laughed. "Deal," she said, tucking the phone in her pocket.

They walked out of the room, much to the joy of the people trying to study amongst Maddie and Nick's giggling and chitchatting.

They walked down the rest of the stairs to the main floor once more. Nick picked up a book from the new arrivals shelf and they walked to the circulation desk.

"Hiya Nick," a middle-aged librarian said to him as he walked up.

"Hey Greta, how are you today?"

"I'm just fine, thanks. How did you like the latest 007 novel?"

"It was just okay," Nick said. "I've read better." The librarian nodded as she checked out the book to him and handed it over, then smiled at Maddie.

"We have one more stop before we go," Nick said, walking with Maddie past the cafe to the gift shop. "You have to pick something out to commemorate your visit, my treat."

"Oh, I couldn't do that," Maddie said. "You've done enough already."

"Don't be daft," Nick said. "Pick out what you want." Maddie's eyes grew wide as she scanned the gift shop. There were lots of little trinkets to choose from. As she meandered through the shop, her gaze fell upon a beautiful cashmere black and white checked scarf. It was an homage to the exhibition that was up about Charles Rennie Mackintosh, a famous Scottish designer. Maddie rubbed the soft fabric between her fingers, then eyed the price tag and moved on. She found a postcard and a magnet that she wanted, and showed them to Nick.

"I found what I want," Maddie said, "But I insist on paying."

"Don't be silly," Nick said, "I think I can handle four pounds." He grabbed the items from Maddie and handed them to the cashier. Maddie stood beside him as the cashier scanned the items, then watched Nick as he turned around and walked through the store. When he came back, he was holding the scarf that she had been looking at.

"Nick—" Maddie began.

"Don't argue with me," Nick said sternly, handing the cashier a wad of cash and grabbing the small bag of trinkets. He pulled out the scarf, gently took the tag off, and wrapped the scarf around her neck. "You need it. It's cold out. An American lass like you can't handle Scotland in January."

How did he do that? How could he do something so sweet one moment and then make her blood positively boil the next?

"Have you ever been to Wisconsin?" Maddie asked him as they walked outside. "It was negative forty degrees last winter. I know a Scotsman like you might not be able to convert Fahrenheit to Celsius, so that's..." Maddie paused to do the calculation of the conversion in her head, then paused again.

"Negative forty in Celsius, too," Nick said, smiling."It's just a coincidence in the conversion." Maddie huffed as they made their way to the truck, scoffing again as Nick held the door open for her.

"You're incorrigible, you know that?" Maddie asked.

"I've been told that before," Nick said, smiling.

As he slid into the truck next to her, Maddie warmed up to him. "I really do love the scarf, Nicholas. That was so sweet of you," she said sincerely.

"You've had a rough go of things," Nick said. "You deserve something to put a smile on your face."

Maddie practically beamed as he said the words. His accent was so strong and so thick that, at times, she feared that she did not understand what he said. This time, though, she heard him perfectly well. He was a good friend, and she was so glad to have met him.

After a few minutes in traffic, they made their way back to the bar. Nick began taking the stools down from the tables and turning the lights on. He started up the grill and began making burgers.

"Who are these for?" Maddie asked. "There's nobody here."

"Well, one's for you," Nick explained as the white apron hugged his body tightly. His flannel sleeves were rolled up, showing some of the tattoos on his arms. "And the rest are for those gents you saw the night you came here. They come every Monday for lunch."

"Ahh, big customers?" Maddie asked as she leaned against the counter and watched him work. The scent of fresh burgers sizzling wafted around her, filling up the kitchen. Her stomach growled as if on cue.

"Some of the only ones," Nick answered. "They are the crew from my Granddad's era," he explained. "Believe it or not, the pub used to be a lot more popular back in the day."

"I believe it," Maddie said. "It's very welcoming, and has a charming vibe," she explained. "Plus, the food is excellent if I do say so myself."

"Thanks, Maddie," Nick said as he put slices of cheddar on the burger. "You might be the only one in your age bracket who thinks so. Just can't keep up with the sports bars and dance clubs I suppose."

"What are you going to do?" Maddie asked.

Nick shrugged as he placed the burgers on buns, then poured fresh fries on the plates next to them. "Keep it going, I suppose."

"I see," Maddie said. Three men walked and Nick greeted them, then set down their food at the booth. Maddie offered to pour their beer for them.

"Have you ever bartended before?" Nick asked as he came around the bar to watch her. Maddie held up a glance to the tapper and shook her head at him.

"No, but I'm a fast learner."

Nick stood behind her and gently clasped her hand that was holding the glass, tipping it slightly to the side. His hand was big and rough, marked with scars. Then he guided her other hand up to the tapper, pressing on it gently. Maddie laughed as the glass filled up, mostly avoiding an overabundance of foam.

Nick quickly dropped his hands as the glass filled up and cleared his throat loudly, tossing a bar towel on his shoulder. "You're a pro now," he said after she filled up two more glasses and delivered them to the men, who eyed her curiously.

"I guess if librarianship doesn't work out I can always be a bartender," she said, smiling.

Nick laughed and sat next to Maddie at the bar, setting their burgers in front of them. The smell was divine, and cheese oozed out from underneath the bun. Maddie used a fry to scoop up some of the extra cheese then popped it in her mouth.

"So, what's your plan?" Nick asked after he took a bite of the burger.

"I guess I don't know," Maddie admitted. "I was hoping to use my time to really see everything Scotland has to offer, but I guess that's not too feasible anymore. To be honest with you, I don't want to go home just yet. I arranged it so that I would leave in two and a half weeks, but I guess I can always try to change my ticket. I am just so mortified by how it all went down with that tool," she confessed. Nick was a good friend, and she trusted him with her true feelings.

"I think I have a solution," Nick said.

"Oh?" Maddie replied. "I couldn't ask you to show me around any more," she said. "I know you have lots of work to do with your woodworking," she explained.

Nick shook his head. "I'm driving the rest of Rosie's things to Inverness before her wedding. If you want to see Scotland, why don't you come on a road trip with me? Once we finish, I can bring you back here to do some more sightseeing. Whatever you'd like."

"Really?" Maddie asked, her eyes wide.

"Really," Nick said, heat growing to his face. "It'll be fun," he said.

With a start, Maddie stood up, pushing the barstool behind her. She jumped to wrap her arms around Nick, then squealed.

"You are the best!" She shouted, grabbing his hairy face between her hands and planting a kiss on his cheek. "What would I do without you?"

Nick's face reddened deeper than ever before after Maddie kissed him. He stood up to his full height next to her, towering above her. Maddie swallowed as he stood next to her, gazing into his eyes. The real question was, what would he do without her?

Chapter 7

Maddie stood in the sitting area of the flat as Nick paced around her, taking artwork off of the walls and carefully preparing it for moving. She watched as his big, hairy hands wrapped the artwork quite delicately, the bubble wrap gently enveloping the artwork.

"Are you sure I can't do anything?" Maddie asked once again, this time getting exasperated.

"No, love," Nick said deeply, looking up from his packing to give her a smile. "I'm almost through."

Maddie looked around the flat and noticed all of the furnishings. "Doesn't she want any of this furniture? Or anything from the kitchen? What about her bed?" Maddie asked, wondering how his sister could be surviving without all of her things.

"She only wants the artwork and a few smaller pieces of furniture," Nick explained, his deep eyes piercing her as he spoke. "The thing is, Rosie is marrying a really wealthy guy. She doesn't exactly need any of this. His house has anything she could ever want and I already built most of that furniture anyway."

Maddie nodded as Nick spoke, wondering what it would be like to be with a wealthy man. She and Melissa did not grow up with much at all and lived in government housing the first half of their lives. While Melissa was now living in Jakob's very large home, Maddie was still in her modest 1970s apartment. She enjoyed it and found that she preferred being cozy and safe to anything else. While she understood the appeal of shacking up with a billionaire, she did not think it was for her. She couldn't even imagine not working at the library for the rest of her life.

Maddie sighed and walked to the kitchen, peering through cupboards while Nick made a pile of items to pack by the door. She heard soft clicks on the window and turned to see snow beginning to fall, hitting the window so hard that it was as if the flakes were not quite sure whether they should be rain or not.

Smiling, Maddie ran to the window. Outside, she saw people walking down the busy street, the snow clinging onto their jackets and hair. The sidewalk began to be covered in white.

"It's snowing, Nick!" Maddie called, a smile in her voice.

Walking up behind her, Nick peered out the window. She could feel his tall body close to hers, and caught the heat emanating from his big body. Maddie found herself holding her breath as she heard his soft breathing behind her. She tried to tuck any feelings of attraction away. Nick was a friend, and literally the opposite of her type.

"Hope it stops soon," Nick said gruffly, grabbing some packing tape from the counter and walking back to a box.

"Don't you like snow?" Maddie asked, turning to face him. She walked over to where he was leaning down over a box, and held the flaps together for him while he taped it shut.

"Don't mind it, I suppose. Just don't feel like traveling in it," he said.

"But the best Hallmark Christmas movies have a snowstorm travel story," Maddie said matter-of-factly. "Don't you watch those all the time?" she teased.

"Oh, you bet I do," Nick said with a smile, lifting up the box effortlessly and taking it over to the door.

Maddie looked around. The flat looked a lot more empty without Rosie's artwork and trinkets. Her phone chirped as she was observing the space. Picking it up from the table, she saw it was her sister who messaged her.

> Melissa: How are you? How is everything? Are you safe?
> Maddie: Hi sis. I am great. I am having such a nice time! Miss you lots.
> Melissa: Is he treating you right? Tell me the truth!
> Maddie: Yes, very well.
> Melissa: Where are you staying?
> Maddie: A flat above a cute little pub called O'Shaughnessy's. I am off to meet his family

soon. Gotta go. Love you!
Melissa: BE CAREFUL! I love you too.

There were only so many fibs that Maddie could tell her sister before completely combusting from lying. She figured that she would mix in a few fibs with some truths. Technically, she was being treated quite right by a man, although it was not the man her sister thought she was with. Additionally, Nick was just a friend. He had to be.

Maddie had always been into the thin, more feminine type of guys. She never really went for beefcakes or guys with tattoos. They were too rough around the edges for her. Although she knew it was a stereotype and a terrible one at that, she was a bit terrified of men who could physically overpower her. She knew that not all men were like her father, but those big muscly men with perpetual scowls always seemed to scare her instead of turning her on.

Interestingly, never once did Nick frighten her. She always felt safe around him, even from the very beginning. Perhaps more than anything, those feelings of safety terrified her. Why would she let her guard down like that? Shaking her head, Maddie set down the phone and looked up to see Nick standing next to a pile of boxes, his elbow propped on the top one as he stood watching her. His enormous, muscled frame was accentuated by one hand casually on his hips.

"Everything okay?" He asked Maddie gently.

"Yes, just fine. It was my sister checking in. Now, I insist you let me help!" Maddie said.

Shaking his head with a smile, Nick handed her a box, which was suspiciously light, and nodded towards the stairs. Maddie sighed as she went forward, then turned back to watch him carrying two large boxes at a time behind her. After scurrying down the steps, they carried the boxes to his truck and began filling up the back.

Maddie rushed back inside before Nick got a chance to stop her and carried some of the heavier boxes down. Nick stood by and raised his eyebrows at that, not saying a word. Between the two of them, everything was soon packed into his truck. It was only early evening by the time they completed, and the snow was still coming down.

"I have to get downstairs to take over for Jimmy," Nick said, his face stretching as he yawned and rubbed his beard. "You should take it easy. We have lots of driving tomorrow. Can I make you some food?" he asked.

"That's nice of you, Nick, but I didn't come all the way to Scotland to sit in an empty flat. Give me a few minutes to freshen up and I'll join you at the pub," Maddie said with a smile.

Nick looked shocked that Maddie wanted to spend more time with him, and simply nodded as he made his way back downstairs. Maddie couldn't help but noticing his firm ass in his tight jeans, swaying gently as he walked away. With a sigh, she shut the door to the flat and spent a few minutes touching up her hair and makeup. Her blonde hair was flattened and frizzy after carrying all the things downstairs, and she tied it into a messy bun in an attempt to look somewhat presentable.

Deciding she would rest for just a moment, Maddie slid her tall body onto one of the white leather chaise lounges and closed her eyes. She found herself thinking of tattoos, and some very particular ones at that. Since Nick nearly always had the sleeves to his flannel shirt rolled up a bit, she was able to notice the intricate designs.

On one arm, his tattoos appeared to be drawings of Grecian or Egyptian women. They were tastefully and respectfully done. One the other arm, she spotted what looked like a family crest. The way the ink weaved and bobbed around his impressively large forearms made deciphering them a little difficult. Maddie made a note to ask him about them and to get a better look sooner rather than later.

Feeling rather frustrated all of a sudden, Maddie grabbed her cell phone and pulled up her Kindle app. She quickly found her favorite erotic romance novel and opened it. It opened right to her go-to sex scene. In it, a mysterious older man meets a gorgeous young woman in a nightclub and takes her under his wing, introducing her to a world of pleasure.

Although Maddie did not think she would like it in real life, the man in the book was very much a dominant. He enjoyed taking control of the woman and making sure she satisfied his every need while also ensuring that she had pleasure after pleasure.

Her Kindle was full of stories similar to these, where powerful men dominated women and claimed them, making them theirs. Whether the novels had red rooms or private jets, she didn't care. Maddie devoured reading about how men stripped women naked, both physically and emotionally, and made them give in to their deep, dark desires.

Before she knew it, Maddie was caught up in the story, her heart beating so fast as she read that she swore she could feel her heart in her throat. With each page, Maddie grew more and more hot, her arousal undeniable. Slowly, gently, she slipped her hand underneath the band of her jeans. Her fingers trailed the lace of her panties before slipping below them, so that nothing came between her and her sex.

As she read about the sexy older man seductively stripping the clothes off of his beautiful woman, Maddie's fingers quickly found her clitoris. With a gasp, she swirled her fingers around, eager to work herself up to a much-needed orgasm.

Maddie's fingers skimmed her hot, silky soft skin and she rubbed her clitoris, both delicately and firmly at the same time. Stifling a moan, she held her phone in one hand and touched herself with the other, allowing herself to be transported to a world where pleasure ruled all.

Maddie greedily rushed her orgasm, feeling the build-up that she craved and desperately reaching for the sweet, sweet relief. With a sigh, she came around her fingers, both arms falling limp as she leaned back and closed her eyes. Without warning, visions of a bearded and tattooed man smattered her imagination, making Maddie's blue eyes shoot open.

What was that about? With a start, she sat up and straightened out her clothes. Tucking her phone into her pocket, she walked to the kitchen and poured herself a glass of water. With a few large gulps, the glass was empty. She set the glass on the counter with a definitive thud and stood peering at the tile floor as if gathering her bearings.

"Get. It. Together," Maddie demanded, tucking a stray lock of blonde hair into her bun and marching towards the door. Shaking her thoughts away, she pattered down the wooden steps down to the bar, hoping there would be something or anything downstairs to distract her from her own thoughts.

Rock music played quietly in the background as Maddie walked through the kitchen and into the bar area. A group of college kids stood around a table, drinking beers and laughing. Maddie was surprised to see anyone under the age of seventy-five in O'Shaughnessy's. The look on her face must have given it away. Nick set down the book he was reading and lazily walked over to her behind the bar.

"I have no idea where they came from either," Nick admitted, a bit of laughter in his eyes.

"Do they know the sports bar is across the street?" Maddie asked, knowing he would find it funny as well.

"I think that their Uber dropped them off at the wrong place. It's the only logical explanation," Nick explained.

"This is great to see," Maddie said seriously. "Maybe things will pick up after all."

"No," Nick said, shaking his head. "It's just a fluke. Business will stay slow. It's just the way things are."

"Oh," Maddie said. She sensed that Nick did not feel like trying too hard to get the pub popular and booming. He seemed content with his crowd of regulars. Maddie couldn't help but wonder why he wouldn't want more. Why wouldn't he want the pub to get more business? Didn't he want it to be successful?

As much as she desperately wanted to know the answers to these questions, she was nowhere near brave enough to ask him about something that she could sense was so immensely personal.

Clearing her throat, Maddie looked up to Nick and asked, "I don't suppose the chef could make me something delicious to eat? I could use a beer, too."

"Anything. Name it," Nick said, reaching over to pick up a glass and filling it with the beer that Maddie liked best.

"As much as I adore your food, I haven't tried any Scottish food since I've been here. Do you have anything that is quintessentially Scottish?"

Nick thought for a moment, then a glimmer of a smile formed in his eyes. "I have just the thing!" He said. "Watch the bar while I go in the back? It will be a while but it will be worth it, love, I promise."

"Sure!" Maddie said as her stomach began to rumble. She was excited to try something new. Nick slid past her, catching her elbow with his hand and giving her a smile.

That flip flop that her stomach just did? Maddie convinced herself it was hunger and nothing else.

Soon, the college kids made their way out and across the street to the club that was booming with people. With a sigh, Maddie collected their empties and began to wash them in the bar sink, sipping on her own beer in the meantime.

Maddie grew anxious as she waited for the food. She was grateful that Nick was cooking for her but also starving. She found a can of peanuts behind the bar and munched on those, watching people walk past the bar, laughing or talking on their phones.

"You doing okay out there?" Nick asked through the kitchen window.

"Just peachy," Maddie said with a smile, reaching for a bottle of vodka and pouring herself a drink.

When she was certain that Nick was not looking, she slipped some money in the cash register, paying for some of the food she had eaten and her drinks.

Delicious smells began to waft from the kitchen. Rich aromas and spices filled the pub and Maddie's mouth practically watered yet again.

Although her patience tested her, Nick soon came out with two steaming plates of food. Maddie was excited as he gestured for her to take a seat at the bar. Setting the plates down next to each other, Maddie was overjoyed as she saw the mound of meat, mashed potatoes, and vegetables.

Holding a finger up as if telling her to wait, Nick jogged back into the kitchen and came out with two glasses of milk. He set them down in front of them, then tore off his apron and set it on the bar. Sitting down next to her, he watched as Maddie inhaled the delicious scents.

"What is this called?" Maddie asked, not sure if even pizza could even compete with this delicacy.

"Haggis, neeps, and tatties," Nick said matter-of-factly, as if that was all the explanation one needed.

"What does any of that mean?" Maddie asked incredulously.

"Meat, turnips, and potatoes," Nick said, taking a sip of milk.

"What kind of meat is haggis?" Maddie asked.

Nick handed her a fork and said, exasperated, "If I explain to you the delicate intricacies of haggis, I guarantee that you won't want to eat it. You Americans are sensitive," he continued.

"Was that really necessary?" Maddie asked, annoyed.

"No, but I enjoy making you all huffy," Nick said with a smile. "Now eat, little one."

Blushing, Maddie began tasting the food, taking bites of each. Hardly able to hold back from shoving as much food in her mouth as possible, she was captivated with the flavors in each of the items. From the spicy meat to the creamy potatoes, she enjoyed every last bit of it.

Before she realized it, her plate was empty and Maddie was stuffed. She and Nick had spent nearly fifteen minutes in silence next to each other, just enjoying the food. Taking a sip of the milk, Maddie grabbed her stomach as she turned on the stool to face him.

"Nicholas!" She exclaimed. "That was the best meal I have ever tasted in my entire life. Where in the world did you learn how to cook?"

Nick blushed, the red creeping up from underneath his sandy beard. "My Mum taught me when I was little. She insisted that we know how to cook. It comes in handy at the pub, but I mostly end up just cooking burgers."

"Is there anything you're not good at?" Maddie asked, completely serious.

Nick considered the question for a moment, then stood up and gathered the plates. He mumbled something under his breath, his Scottish accent too strong for Maddie to make it out. She jumped up from the barstool and followed him into the kitchen. "What was that?" She asked, wishing he would repeat what he said.

He began washing the pots and pans, along with the dishes, and let out an exasperated sigh. "If you must know," Nick said, "It's women. I'm bad at women."

"How is that even remotely possible?" Maddie asked, incredulously. She strode over to the sink and began helping him scrub the pans. They worked into a system, her washing, him rinsing.

"What do you mean?" Nick asked.

"Well, for one, you're fucking gorgeous," Maddie admitted. "Two, you're really nice. And three, you have extreme cooking talent. What woman wouldn't want you?"

"Lots of them, apparently," Nick muttered, stacking up plates to be dried.

"I don't buy it," she said, continuing to scrub the pans.

"Well, it's the truth," Nick admitted.

"How long have you been single?" she asked him, finishing up the pans and moving to the other side of him to grab a clean towel to begin drying.

"I don't know, a while," he admitted. "What about you? What are you doing messing around with idiots like Calum when there are dozens of better men?"

"Oh no," Maddie said defiantly. "Don't you turn this around on me. We are talking about you, mister!" she said.

With a shrug, Nick began putting away the pans that Maddie dried. "I've always had a hard time with women," Nick admitted. "I guess I've never met one who I really click with. Don't get me wrong, I love women and I have the utmost respect for them, but I suppose nobody has ever come along who made me want to be with them seriously."

"Well, I can understand that," Maddie admitted. She had never had a boyfriend. If she was being honest, Calum was the closest she had ever gotten to one. With that so very clearly off the table, where did that leave her at twenty-six?

"You deserve everything and more," Nick said, pulling the towel out of her hand and tossing it on the counter. Slowly, his rough hand clutched her chin, tilting it up to face him. "Promise me one thing. Promise me you'll never settle for anything less than what you deserve."

With a hard gulp, Maddie found her voice somewhere deep inside of her to say what came next. "I promise," she said quietly, really meaning it.

Returning His Love

Chapter 8

After finishing up in the kitchen, the two went upstairs . Maddie agreed when Nick asked if they could get an early start on their road trip. Nick explained that, while he was gone, the bar would just be closed for the duration. Maddie found it hard to sleep and was tossing and turning. She could hear the soft sounds of Nick walking around in the flat above. How could she possibly sleep when Nick was so clearly wide awake?

Eventually, the lull of sleep got to her and she was able to catch a few hours of sleep before waking up long before her alarm and double-checking her suitcase to ensure that she packed everything.

This was ridiculous, she realized. First she traveled halfway across the world to meet a stranger. That clearly worked out so well, so why not travel halfway across Scotland with another man—a big one, at that?

The anticipation of spending so much time with Nick alone made her a bit nervous. They were friends, just friends, she reassured herself. A rap on her door took her out of her own thoughts and Maddie slid on her leather jacket. It paired well with her light skinny jeans and black booties.

Wheeling her suitcase to the door, Maddie took a breath and looked around the flat one more time. After delivering Nick's sister's things, she would probably stay here a few more times, but she was going to miss the cozy flat and the extra comfortable bed.

Opening the door, Maddie found Nick in a light blue down jacket, holding two travel mugs of steaming hot coffee. Outstretching one to her, she nearly salivated at its decadent smell.

"I couldn't sleep last night," Nick said. "So I got up early and got us some coffee."

"Thank you!" Maddie exclaimed. reaching out to take the coffee. Her hands instantly warmed up from the mug, and she shivered a little.

Nick took the handle of her bag and carried it downstairs. Maddie locked the door to the flat and followed him. They went through the darkened, empty pub and ensured that it, too, was locked up.

The blast of cold air hit Maddie without warning. Her face was instantly frozen and her teeth chattered together. Nick's pickup was parked on the street, engine on and exhaust pumping. Nick set down her suitcase on the deserted sidewalk and nodded his head to the passenger door. Holding it open for her, Maddie slid past him and into the truck, instantly enveloped in heat.

Not only was heat pumping through the vents but her seat was heated as well. She warmed up in no time.

After storing her bags in the back, Nick came around and climbed into the drivers' side of the vehicle. The cold emanated off of his body. He rubbed his big hands together before taking a sip of his coffee. Turning to Maddie, he asked her in a deep, gravelly voice, "Ready to see Scotland?"

"Yes!" Maddie said assuredly, tightening her seatbelt as Nick took off into the early morning. The Sun wasn't even up yet. Shops were still closed, save for a few coffee places. The darkness of the city invigorated Maddie. She wanted to explore everything this country had to offer. While she did like the hustle and bustle of Glasgow, she was looking forward to seeing the countryside.

Ever since she was a little girl, Maddie itched to see the world. The only time she got to explore new places was in library books. She recalled hours spent at the public library exploring books about different countries, wishing she could escape and visit them all.

Looking back, there was nothing pleasant about her childhood. While she had good memories of fun times with Melissa, she realized now that most of that fun was had in order to distract her from what was really going on. An abusive, alcoholic father and a mother who was desperate to try to escape the situation was not a pleasant way to grow up, but Melissa always tried to protect her from what was really going on.

One day, of course, Melissa couldn't protect her sister anymore and that's when their mother died, trying to pull their drunken father off of Maddie as he beat her. When he stopped beating Maddie to push their mother off of him, she tumbled down the stairs. Even the villain himself was silent for a moment when she fell in a heap on the first floor.

Maddie knew just how much Melissa had given up to protect her. She had to mature much too fast in order for Maddie to be able to have some semblance of a childhood. In the pictures that do exist from that time, they always managed to have huge smiles on their faces. Maddie did have lots of time away from their father, with dozens of trips to the library and the park, Melissa always holding her hand. If it wasn't for Melissa, Maddie mused, she had no idea where she would be now.

Shaking the memories out of her mind, Maddie glanced at the clock on the truck and realized that they had been driving for fifteen minutes already. Now on a highway, Maddie glanced over at Nick, who was stealing looks at her as he concentrated on the road.

"Sorry I disappeared for a bit," Maddie said, clearing her throat.

"Driving always gives a person time to think," Nick nodded, giving her a quiet smile.

"What do you think about?" Maddie asked, wanting to take her mind off of her own thoughts.

"The past, mostly," Nick said quietly, reaching down for his coffee. Taking a swig, he turned off onto a country road. The sun was beginning to come up, frost and snow covering the farmland. "You?"

"Same," Maddie said quietly. "Do you ever have a memory that ruins your entire day?"

"Far too often," Nick nodded, locking eyes with her. His deep blue eyes were even more piercing today, and Maddie tried to force off a shiver when he looked at her.

"Any tips on blocking them out of your mind forever?" Maddie asked humorously.

"I wish I did. If I knew, you'd be the first person I'd tell," he replied solemnly. "I wouldn't wish what you've been through on my worst enemy."

Maddie nodded. Quietly, she explained a bit more to Nick about her past, bringing up some details that she wish she would never have to speak about again. Nick's hands grew tight on the steering wheel once more, his eyes staring too intently at the road.

"I have Melissa. Not everybody is so lucky to have such a great sibling. She is so happy with Jakob. It makes me smile when I see them together. They are like a couple in a romance novel or something. You can just tell they are meant to be," Maddie said with a sigh, her breath catching as she thought about it.

"It sounds like Rosie and her fiancé. She lights up just talking about him. I am so happy she found someone who treats her well," Nick explained.

"Isn't that every big brother's dream for his little sister?" Maddie asked, smiling now.

"If it's not, it should be," Nick said gruffly, his protective mode in full swing.

"You're pretty cute when you get all big brother, you know," Maddie said with a laugh.

A blush creeped up past Nick's beard and painted his cheeks pink. With a laugh, he looked out his window and smiled, saying nothing in reply.

"So it's just you and Rosie, huh?" Maddie asked him, not letting Nick get away with being shy.

Silently, he nodded. "You'll get to meet most of my family when we arrive," he explained. "Rosie will be excited to meet you."

"Oh?" Maddie asked inquisitively. "When's the last time you brought a woman to meet your family?"

"Senior prom," Nick answered.

"High school?" Maddie's eyes opened incredulously. "That's like," she paused while doing the mental math, "twenty years ago! What gives?"

Nick shrugged. "What do you mean?"

"You haven't brought a woman to meet your family in twenty years!" Maddie repeated. "Why not?"

Nick gave her an absent stare, as if he had no idea what the issue was.

"I get that you're a bit of a hermit," Maddie began, "And that's totally cool. I like to not leave my house, too. But have you taken a look in the mirror lately?" She asked incredulously.

"What does that have to do with anything?" he asked, now starting to get defensive.

Maddie sat up in her seat, moving so that her entire body faced Nick.

"Nicholas!" she exclaimed. "You are a stone cold fox. Not only do you have a body only rivaled by Greek Gods, but you have this magnificent beard and blue eyes that can only accurately be compared to the Aegean Sea! Plus, you're the fucking nicest guy I've met in a long time and you can cook. Give me one good reason why you should be single," Maddie prodded.

Nick took his eyes off of the road long enough to search Maddie's face, as if wondering if she was being genuine or just teasing him. After seeing her imploring eyes, desperate for an answer from him, Nick knew that she was serious. However, he could not possibly know where to go from there.

"We all have our demons," Nick said gruffly, but gently. Maddie reached out and grabbed his hand that was resting on his thigh. She captured the big hand, with roughened fingertips and short, clean nails, and gave it a tight squeeze. For just a moment, her small, pale hand enveloped his.

"I know," Maddie said quietly. She could sense his entire body tensing as she took Nick's hand in her own. After lazily tracing her thumb over his hand, she moved to release it, not wanting to extend the moment too long. She couldn't send the wrong message to Nick. They were just friends.

As she began to pull her hand away, Nick reached out and grabbed it, now taking her hand in his. He pulled her hand up to his mouth, feeling the scruff of his beard on her fingertips. Quickly, quietly, he placed a kiss on the back of her hand.

Maddie bit back a moan. This was just like in the novels. He gently set her hand down and went back to focusing on the road. After a minute or two of complete and total silence, in which Maddie had about three panic attacks in her mind, Nick said, "You think my eyes are nice, huh?"

With a smile, Maddie looked at him. "The best," she said. "We'll find you a girl to bring home to your Mom yet."

"What about you?"

"What about me?" Maddie asked incredulously. "We are just friends. You're not my type."

"But you said I have a nice beard, too," Nick said with a smile.

"Well, yeah, you are totally hot!" Maddie explained. "But I don't really go for such masculine guys. Give me skinny jeans and a man bun any damn day."

With a grunt, Nick muttered something under his breath.

"What was that?" Maddie asked.

"Nothing," he said gruffly.

"Tell me, I insist," Maddie said.

A moment passed before Nick pulled off of the highway and drove into a small town. He parked in front of a small cafe and turned to Maddie.

"What has going after men who wear fookin' skinny jeans and buns in their hair gotten you, Maddie? Are men like Calum MacGregor really what you want? Is that truly what you think you deserve? To be treated like shite?" Nick chastised her firmly but not unkindly, and Maddie knew.

Looking downwards, Maddie realized that he was right. Going after the men that she had always been attracted to really was not working for her, and she felt foolish about everything that went down with Calum. She hated that Nick was right, and did not want to admit it. However, after everything he had done for her, she supposed that he at least deserved her honesty.

"You're right," Maddie said, a tear beginning to fall from her eyes.

"Oh, love," Nick said, unbuckling his seatbelt and leaning in closer to her. "I am so sorry! I did not mean to make you cry.

"It wasn't you," Maddie said. "You were just saying the truth. It's me. I wish I didn't make such stupid decisions. If you must know, I've never had a boyfriend. I mean, I guess I thought that Calum was my boyfriend but we all know how well that ended. It really just stems to me being so stupid about men. I like to think I am a smart person. I have a Master's Degree for God's sake. I guess I am just one of those people who is book smart but has complete lack of any social awareness. I should just stick to romance novels," Maddie said dejected. She had stopped crying by now, and was nothing but embarrassed.

"You are smart, Maddie. It's not your fault that Calum pulled one over on you. He's been a bad apple from the start. I am sorry I said anything. I shouldn't have."

"You are right, though," Maddie said with a sigh. I shouldn't be so particular with what I like. Maybe that's half my problem."

Nick shrugged. "You like what you like, can't help that."

"I suppose," Maddie said. For the first time she took a look at their surroundings. "Where are we?"

"Our first stop of the trip is Stirling. It's the meeting ground of the highlands and lowlands. I figured we could stop for breakfast and I'll show you the castle."

"There's a castle?" Maddie asked excitedly. Quickly forgetting their conversation just moments ago, Maddie opened her door and jumped out of the truck. As she stood on the brick road, which hardly had any traffic at the early hour, she looked up. There, on a tall mountain covered in trees, stood a behemoth of a castle.

Maddie practically swooned at the sight of it. The enormous gray structure seemed to be larger than life. Quite literally erected from the stone of the mountains, the castle looked both ominous and romantic in the early morning sunlight. She could hardly catch her breath as she looked up at the mountain, dying to get a chance to see inside.

"It's so beautiful!" Maddie exclaimed as Nick came up and stood next to her. "Can you believe that you live in such a beautiful country all the time? You are so lucky," she said, pulling out her phone to snap a few photos. Realizing that she was cold, Maddie shivered a bit before Nick gestured to a coffeehouse. Holding the door open for her, Maddie smiled up at Nick as she walked inside.

The smell of strong coffee and breakfast food wafted into Maddie's nostrils. As if on command, her stomach growled. She smiled as she noticed the tartan carpeting. The small shop's walls were all stone, and it gave her a cozy feeling. A plump woman with a green apron on came over to greet Nick and Maddie and she quickly found them a table.

The cafe was surprisingly busy for it being only seven o'clock in the morning. They spent a few minutes looking over the menu. Maddie was not sure what she wanted, everything looking so much like what she could get in the States. "I want something Scottish," Maddie said assuredly. "What would that be?" When the woman came back to take their order, Nick handed the menus to her and said, "We'll have two full Scottish breakfasts."

"Coming right up," the woman said cheerily.

"That sounds like a lot of food. It wasn't even on the menu," Maddie said.

"You like food," Nick said matter-of-factly.

"That's true," Maddie said. "But what if I don't like it?"

"I guarantee you will like at least part of this," Nick said.

"Or what?"

"If you don't like *anything* they serve you, I will find and drink one of those disgusting green drinks you American girls are so fond of toting around."

Maddie sat back in her chair and laughed. Just when she thought that Nick was the type of person to not pay attention to little things like green smoothies, he surprised her with his humor.

The woman brought a pot of tea over and two mugs. She set another pot down as well. Maddie poured herself some of the tea and filled Nick's cup too, inhaling the strong scent.

"What's in the other pot?" Maddie asked Nick.

"Water," he responded. "You might want to—"

Not waiting for him to finish, Maddie blew on her tea to cool it off and took a big sip. With a grimace, Maddie reluctantly swallowed the piping hot tea. "Why is it so strong?" she whispered.

"That's what the water is for," Nick said, pouring some of the water in his mug before taking a sip.

"I see," Maddie said with pursed lips. "Never was much of a tea gal myself."

Laughing, Nick smiled. Soon, the kind waitress set two steaming bowls of porridge in front of them.

"Okay, this I can handle," Maddie said confidently. While she was used to instant oatmeal, this porridge was decadently rich with flavor. They sat quietly and enjoyed the porridge. Just when Maddie was about finished, the waitress brought out a rack of toast and marmalade.

"Oh there's more?" Maddie asked, clearly overwhelmed by the amount of food. "I guess I shouldn't have eaten all that porridge."

"We Scots know how to deliver," Nick said with a wink. Maddie munched on toast lathered with sweet marmalade, her eyes growing wide as the waitress came to their table yet again.

She set two plates in front of them. They both were filled to the brim with food. Maddie could have sworn that she had never seen such a breakfast in her life.

The plate held a sliced tomato with cheese, bacon, a scone of some sort, a sausage link, mushrooms, beans, a fried egg, and a dark object that resembled a hockey puck. Maddie gulped as she took in all the food. "We aren't at IHOP anymore," she said under her breath.

Nick pointed to the scone. That's a tattie scone—made with potato." Then he pointed to the hockey puck. "Do you know what that is?"

"No," Maddie said, picking up her fork.

"It's blood pudding," he explained. "It's pork and oats."

"Sounds...delicious," Maddie said. Taking a small bite of the pudding, Maddie was pleasantly surprised. "I'm impressed," she said.

"You like it then?" Nick asked with a smile.

"Rest assured, there will be no green drinks for you." Smiling, Nick picked up his fork and began to eat, his eyes mischievous as he watched Maddie.

After they finished their meal, Maddie sat back in the chair and clutched her stomach. "That was amazing!" she said. "I'll never doubt your breakfast choices again."

"Thanks, love," Nick said. He placed some bills on the table and then stood up. His tall frame extended to its full height as he stretched. Maddie couldn't resist her eyes roaming up and down his body. She could not deny that Nick was built, with big, burly arms and a trim torso. He had a great body, yet was not cocky about it. If anything, he covered it up.

Nick was wearing a pair of Levi's and a green flannel shirt. While he tugged on his down jacket, he smiled as Maddie stood up and zipped up her jacket. She wrapped the scarf that Nick gave her around her neck. Nick watched as she carefully tied the scarf, his eyes growing hooded as he observed her careful movements. Clearing his throat abruptly, Nick guided Maddie out of the restaurant. She began walking towards the truck but Nick called out after her.

"We aren't taking that," Nick said.

"How are we going to get up the mountain then? Listen, Nick, we don't all have calves of steel. I am not walking!" Maddie replied firmly.

With a wink, Nick put his arm around Maddie's shoulder and steered her in the opposite direction. "We aren't walking, I promise," he reassured her.

'Thank God," she muttered. They walked down the cobblestone streets and Maddie found herself enthralled by the little town. Shops with artisan products in the window called her name, and Maddie wished she could come back when they were open.

Soon, they came to a small building. Outside the building, a miniature green train was parked. "What's this?" Maddie asked excitedly. The train looked like an old-fashioned locomotive yet on a much smaller scale. It had benches that could fit about twenty or so people. Maddie was thrilled at the chance to ride it and felt like a kid again.

"We are going to take this up the hill to get to the castle," Nick said. "Are you excited?"

"Are you kidding me?" she practically squealed. "This is the coolest thing ever!"

They waited around a few minutes until the driver came. He began setting up and getting the train ready to go. A school bus pulled into the parking lot and a crowd of nuns fanned out of it and surrounded them. They pushed past Nick and Maddie, who were stunned silent, and settled into the train. They were smiling and laughing ecstatically, chattering about.

The driver looked at Nick and Maddie after the nuns got settled. "Looks like there's only one spot left," he said, nodding to the caboose. Nick looked over to Maddie, who was trying not be crushed about it.

"It's okay," Maddie said. "We can always come back another time. I know you need to get your sister her things, anyway."

"Not a chance," Nick said, grabbing Maddie's hand and pulling her over to the caboose. He took a seat next to a thin, elderly nun, who Maddie could have sworn was blushing as she stared at Nick and adjusted her habit. Looking at Maddie, he grabbed her by the hips and pulled her into his lap, her legs swinging out from the caboose.

"Nicholas!" Maddie shouted. "This is ridiculous. I am much too heavy. Put me down this instant." The more she struggled, the tighter his grip became. His big arms wrapped around her waist, firmly gripping Maddie.

Maddie suddenly felt warm as the nuns chattered and eyed the two of them. She reached to pull the scarf away from her neck, loosening it. Turning to Nick, she realized that she was much closer to his face than she had ever been before. When she caught his gaze, Nick's Adam's apple bobbed up and down. The closer she was to Nick, the more she could see the smattering of freckles on his face, and the tiny wrinkles around his eyes and mouth. He was, Maddie determined, a very attractive man.

Maddie could feel the heat emanating from his body, his hands practically burning her hips as they grazed below her jacket. "I've got you, love," Nick said firmly.

"You're the sweetest man I've ever met," Maddie said honestly. "Is there anything you wouldn't do to make me happy?"

"I can't think of a thing," Nick replied, his voice deep and pure.

The moment was broken as the conductor dramatically shouted, "All aboard!" The nuns screeched with excitement and Maddie couldn't help but laugh. As they began driving down the road and came closer to the mountain, Maddie's pulse raced. The more the train wobbled, the harder Nick held tight to her. She had never been so close to a man before, and she couldn't help but admit that it felt wonderful.

The sweet, cinnamon smell mixed with a deep pine that emanated from Nick would have made her knees weak if Maddie was not already sitting down. It was one of the most masculine scents that she had ever had the pleasure of being exposed to, and she swore that as long as she lived, she would never forget it.

Chapter 9

As they made their way up the hill, the view of the city stunned Maddie. It looked just like the pictures that she saw in books. It was the little village that she dreamed about escaping to as a child. Being here with Nick was everything.

Coming closer to the castle, Maddie discovered that it was even bigger than she imagined. The enormous structure greeted them as they went over a small bridge and parked in front of the castle.

Maddie gingerly stood up from Nick's lap, careful not to hit her head on the roof of the caboose. She felt Nick's hand on her hip as he helped her out. Maddie watched Nick climb his way out of the caboose, the nuns standing around watching him as he stretched to his full height. She could have sworn that they sighed as he lifted his hand to rub his beard and a bit of his torso peaked out from under his jacket. Maddie couldn't blame them.

They followed the guide to the front of the castle. Maddie pulled out her phone to snap some photos. "I've always wanted to stay in a castle, preferably one that's a little bit haunted," Maddie said to Nick as they made their way into the castle after the nuns.

"Lots of these castles have ghosts," Nick said. "Aren't you scared?"

"Of ghosts? Nah," Maddie said courageously. She gasped as she stepped into the main hall. The beautiful decorations were deliciously regal, with huge tapestries boasting coats of arms hanging over fireplaces and portraits climbing the walls of the staircase of people long gone.

They made their way through the tour, Maddie more and more excited with every room they went in. Nick snapped a few photos of Maddie. She was in heaven.

"It's so beautiful," she murmured as she walked down the stairs.

"Would you like me to take your photo?" A tall nun walked over to them, her arm extended to take their phone. Nick and Maddie looked at each other as they stood outside the castle. Nick shrugged his shoulders and Maddie nodded.

They stood outside the castle and smiled as the nun walked backwards with Maddie's phone. "Stand closer together," she shouted to them. Maddie looked at Nick, who was standing stoically a foot away from her. She reached out and wrapped her hands around his arm. Nick smiled and moved to put his arm around her waist. They looked towards the nun and smiled for a few pictures.

A younger nun came up and looked at them. "Give 'er a smooch!" she shouted.

"Sister Irene!" The older one chastised.

"They may as well have a little fun!" Irene explained.

Before she knew what was happening, Nick leaned down and kissed Maddie on the cheek.

"Got it!" The older nun cheered as she handed the phone back to Maddie. The entire cheek that Nick kissed was tingling. Maddie had to force herself not to raise her hand to her cheek to touch the spot that Nick kissed. She avoided eye contact with him as she slipped the phone in her pocket and followed him over to a pasture.

A tall man with red hair who looked to be about Nick's age was walking out of a barn. Behind him, two baby highland cattle waddled out unsteadily. Maddie gasped as she saw the furry little creatures, practically jumping up and down.

The man spotted Nick and called out, "Eh, O'Shaughnessy is it? How are you, mate?" Nick called back at him and the man told them to come into the gated area. Maddie followed Nick and, after ensuring that she closed the gate, practically ran over to the calves.

"May I?" Maddie asked.

"Sure thing, lass," the friendly man said. He handed her a bottle. "You can feed them if you'd like."

"Really?" Maddie asked incredulously. Her eyes grew wide. She sat on the frozen ground and let the calves come up to her. With a laugh, she gingerly began feeding one, the other fighting for a turn with the bottle.

Laughing, Maddie played with the cattle as Nick stood aside, talking fast in his Scottish accent with his friend. She wasn't really paying attention, but from what she could gather, they seemed to be insulting each other the entire time yet in a cheerful tone. Was this the Scottish way? It sure seemed to be.

"Who's your lass?" the man asked.

"This is Maddie," Nick said. "She's on holiday from the States."

"Nice to meet you, Maddie," the man said as he crouched down to play with one of the calves. "The name is Bob. I've known your man O'Shaughnessy here since he was a wee boy."

Instead of correcting his friend, Maddie just laughed and said, "I find it hard to believe that Nicholas was ever little."

With a laugh, Bob slapped his thigh and smiled. "You know him well. O'Shaughnessy has always been a thick man."

Maddie laughed as the calves emptied the bottle. Standing up, Maddie smiled at Bob. "It was so nice to meet you. Thank you so much for letting me play with the calves. They are adorable."

"Anytime, lass. You take care of my mate, okay?" Maddie smiled and nodded. The two walked out of the pasture and over to the other side of the castle. It overlooked an enormous, hilly countryside filled with trees. Maddie could have sworn that she was Catherine in *Wuthering Heights*.

"So are we just going to let all your friends and the nuns think we are a couple?" Maddie asked Nick as she snapped photos of the countryside.

"That's the plan," Nick said.

"Oh yeah?" Maddie said with a smile. "Why is that?"

"I have no trouble letting all of my old mates think that I am with a beautiful woman. You don't mind, do you?" Nick asked, now worried that he overstepped.

"Not at all!" Maddie said. "I can be your pretend girlfriend any day!" They walked along the hills for a little while longer until they heard the roar of the train start up. As they piled into the train once more, Nick avoided eye contact as Maddie sat on his lap again. He didn't speak to her once, and Maddie worried that she did something wrong. The trip down the hill was quiet, with Maddie listening to the nuns and their hilarious conversations about Father Richard's ridiculous antics.

Once safely down the hill, Maddie slid off of Nick's lap. She looked over at him and he had a pained expression on his face, choosing once more to avoid looking at her. They walked back to the truck in silence. Finally, once they were buckled in, Maddie said, "What did I do?"

Nick appeared startled as he looked over at her. "What are you talking about?" he asked.

"It's like a switch went off or something. You didn't talk or look at me the entire way down. Do I smell or something?" she asked, sticking her hand into her jacket to see if her armpits were sweaty.

"Not at all," Nick said. In fact, she was the opposite of smelly. "You smell like soft spring days and honeysuckle. You smell like perfection," Nick said stoically.

Maddie slapped Nick's thigh and started laughing at his description of her. "That's oddly specific," she said, laughing and blushing.

"It's the truth," Nick said, blushing himself behind his beard.

"Well, what is it then? Are you freaking out about the whole pretending to be dating thing?" Maddie asked, desperate to talk about anything other than what she smelled like.

"No," Nick said assuredly. "It's not that."

"Well, what the hell?" Maddie said exasperatedly. "You've gotta tell me what's up."

Nick tilted his head back and sighed, closing his eyes, just as he did when she sat on his lap on the train ride back. He began to mutter under his breath once more, and Maddie sighed heavily.

"If you must know," he said, not moving from his position, his eyes still closed, "I was trying to control myself."

"Control yourself? What do you mean? Were those nuns really annoying you that much?"

"Well they were," Nick mused, "but that's not what I mean."

"Tell me," Maddie insisted once more.

"You really have no idea of the effect you have on men, do you?" Nick asked incredulously.

Maddie stared at Nick as he tilted his head up and gazed at her. "Here I am, trying to keep my cool with a gorgeous woman in my lap. I am one wrong thought away from embarrassing myself in front of you and two dozen nuns."

"Keep your cool?" Maddie asked. Realization set in. "Oh. *Ohhhh*," she said, nodding. "I suppose that's just a reaction that most men can't control, eh?" She mused. "Probably would have happened if Sister Irene sat in your lap, huh?" Maddie was genuinely curious. She was by no means an expert on boners.

Nick practically spit out the water he was gulping as he looked over at her. "I can guarantee that Sister Irene would not have given me the same reaction," Nick said. "We talked about the type of guy you like, right? Do you want to know my type?"

"Sure," Maddie said, leaning forward. Now she was curious.

"Tall, overly-friendly blonde librarians with stunning blue eyes and pert arses," Nick said. Maddie's eyes grew wide.

"Shit," Maddie said. "That's me," she said, staring out of the front window as she bit on her lip.

"That's you," Nick said.

"But we are just friends," Maddie insisted. "Friends who occasionally pretend to be dating, but that's it. That's as far as it can go, right?"

"Yes," Nick insisted. "I'm far too old for you, anyway. And I'm not looking for a woman. I am better alone. Plus, you're going back home soon. We *are* just friends."

Maddie nodded as Nick started up the engine and pulled away from the curb. She flipped on the radio to a rock station and they drove in silence as Maddie sent her sister some of the photos, her hand shaking as she selected them on her phone.

Nick merged onto the highway, A9, and Maddie focused on the views. The highlands were gorgeous.

Rolling hills and beautiful frost-tipped trees surrounded them. She had never witnessed such captivating scenery in her entire life. To Nick, this scenery was just another day in the life. To Maddie, the views were a once-in-a-lifetime experience.

Instead of falling into a comfortable silence, which oftentimes happened between the two, Maddie decided to chatter on about life back home. She talked about her work and being a librarian, telling Nick some hilarious stories about patrons. Nick smiled as she told the stories.

Maddie ventured into her war stories about storytimes and that led to a conversation about fairytales. "I know it's naive," Maddie said. "But I've never stopped believing in fairytales. Melissa always laughs at me because I am never not reading a romance novel. I suppose I realize that it's fictional, but I just want that true love."

Nick tore his eyes from the road to look at Maddie, then reached out to tuck a lock of hair behind her ear. "You'll find it, I am certain of it," he said seriously.

"And a super romantic proposal, too, of course," Maddie said. "A springtime wedding. Doesn't that sound perfect?" she said, allowing herself to fantasize. "I'd love to live in a big old farmhouse and have dogs running around."

"You'd make a beautiful bride, love," Nick said, quietly taking a sip of the now-cold coffee.

How could a girl not smile at that? Maddie was entirely enjoying the flirtation with Nick, finding herself more and more attracted to the man who she initially only saw as a brute and nothing else.

Instead of letting Nick get away with too much silence, Maddie then began prodding him with questions. She quickly found out that his favorite color was green, just like hers, and that his middle name was Reginald. After snorting with laughter at her discovery, Maddie shared her own middle name.

"My Mom really liked that old Hitchcock movie, *Rebecca*, so that's my middle name. Kind of a spooky namesake if you ask me," she said before continuing on to ask him more questions and prod him into pronouncing random words in "Scottish."

"You do know that's not a language, right?" Nick asked with a grin.

"It sounds like a foreign language most of the time!" Maddie replied.

"Don't get me started on you Americans again," Nick said gruffly. Maddie smiled at that, enjoying teasing him.

They were on the highway for half an hour when Maddie finished up telling her sister and Jakob's love story. She sighed contentedly just thinking about it. After breakfast and the tour, it was already nearly noon. They pulled up to a gas station and Nick jumped out to fill up the gas tank. Maddie went into the gas station to use the bathroom.

In the small gas station mirror, she attempted to fix her windblown hair, but it was hopeless at this point. She grabbed two sodas and a bag of chips before leaving the store and paid for Nick's gas before he had a chance to come inside.

She waited for him while he used the bathroom, opening the bag of chips and beginning to munch on them. While he went up to pay for the gas, the attendant told him that she had already paid.

Nick turned towards her and shook his head. Before giving him a chance to complain about her paying, Maddie held out a soda and gave him a sweet smile. "That's what friends are for," she said, rushing back out to the truck.

Chapter 10

The rest of the drive was quiet, the two making conversation about Nick's woodworking as they drove their way to the next stop. They pulled off the highway with signs directing them to Dahlwinnie. Maddie could hardly wait to see what was next on her tour of Scotland.

The views were absolutely breathtaking. The longer they traveled, the more hilly and craggy the roads became. Dozens of lakes surrounded the roads, and there was wildlife just about everywhere. From birds flying high to cows on the side of the road, Maddie was enthralled.

"Where are we going next?" Maddie asked Nick.

"I'm taking you to Cairngorms National Park," Nick explained. "It's got some beautiful views."

"I am so pumped!" Maddie exclaimed. "We are basically in an episode of *Outlander* right now."

Nick rolled his eyes at that remark. "Right," he said, "Definitely."

"Don't tell me you don't watch that show," Maddie teased.

"Believe it or not, Maddie, I don't," he said.

They gained entry to the park and Nick pulled into a parking spot. They found a trail and began to walk. The sounds of nature and wildlife, from birds chirping to wind blowing through the trees, was so strong. Maddie became immersed in the experience and enjoyed seeing the hilly countryside as they walked.

They did not go too far on the trail, just enough to really see the hills and mountains. "It's gorgeous!" Maddie said excitedly.

"I knew you'd like this place," Nick said. "I used to come here with—" he paused, then decided against finishing his sentence. "I have lots of good memories here," Nick said. "Why don't we go grab some lunch?"

Maddie sensed his discomfort. "That sounds like great idea," Maddie said, and after taking one last look at the view, they made their way down the hill and back to the park's entrance.

They found an Italian restaurant near the park and Maddie eagerly agreed to split a pizza with Nick. She had no trouble admitting that she had an addiction to pizza and could hardly wait to get home just to order some from her favorite place.

Soon, their pizza was delivered to the table. Maddie's half had just cheese, whereas Nick's half was topped with everything imaginable, including anchovies.

"You're disgusting," Maddie joked as she watched him eat the pizza.

"You're the one who doesn't even like toppings," he teased.

"You have a point," Maddie said, her mouth full of pizza. If there was one thing Maddie was good at, it was throwing down half a pizza. For a trim person, the girl could eat. Where it all went was a mystery.

Nick watched astonishingly as she easily ate just as much as him and shook his head, a twinkle in his eyes.

After they finished their food, Maddie looked at Nick with puppy dog eyes. "I know we have to get going," Maddie said, "And I am so grateful that you took the time to show me this special park," she continued. "Do you think we could spend just a little more time here before we take off?" Maddie asked, plastering a smile on her face.

"Anything you want," Nick said, following Maddie as she practically skipped out of the restaurant. She found a hilly pasture near the parking lot. She began to walk up the hill and zipped her jacket, feeling the brisk wind of the cold January day.

Maddie ran along until she came upon a cliff. Birds chirped around her as she stood, overlooking a beautiful lake which was iced over in some spots. Across from the lake stood dozens of hills, the landscape more beautiful than she could even imagine.

Nick made his way next to her and they stood in silence for a few moments. Maddie sighed, then turned around and eyed the craggy terrain that she walked up. She hipped and hopped her way down. Turning to look back at Nick, who was watching her intently, the wind was knocked out of her as she tripped over a huge rock.

As she fell, Maddie muttered dozens of curse words. Her ankle twisted as she tried to stop her fall and, as she hit the ground, she knew it was all over.

"Maddie!" Nick shouted as he came up next to her. "Are you all right, love?"

Pain shot through her ankle as Maddie tried to keep a straight face. She assessed her pain and recognized that she had royally messed something up. Pain seared up her leg as she groaned and sat up, reaching for her bootie.

"Wait!" Nick stopped her. "Don't pull off the shoe until we know what's happened," Nick said. "You don't want to hurt it more." Maddie sighed as Nick touched her ankle.

"Fook!" He muttered under his breath. Swearing once more, Nick swept his arms underneath Maddie and picked her up effortlessly.

She didn't have the energy to stop him as tears came to her eyes from the pain. Nick's face was scrunched in worry as he hurried down the hill so fast that it was as if he wasn't even carrying her.

When they made it to the parking lot, Nick held her with one arm as he opened the door and set her gingerly in the truck. Maddie swiped a tear from her eyes as Nick rushed over to the other side and started the truck. He sped down the hilly road to the main entrance of the park and threw the truck in park in front of the ranger's office.

Nick came around and picked Maddie up once again, carrying her into the office. The rangers directed them to a first aid office. A nurse came in and listened to

Nick explain what happened. She nodded as she listened. Looking towards Maddie, she began gently pulling off her bootie and inspected her ankle, which was swollen. Nick stood in the corner of the examination room, fear in his eyes and the nurse poked and prodded her ankle. She had Maddie sit up and put weight on the ankle. She was able to walk, although it hurt.

"It's a bad sprain," the nurse asserted. I will wrap it up and you should stay off of it for a day or so."

"How can you be so sure it's not broken or something else?" Nick asked fervently. "Should we take her to the hospital for scans?"

"If it was broken, she wouldn't be able to put weight on it," the nurse said calmly as she wrapped the ankle. "I wouldn't risk putting these boots back on," she said. Maddie nodded and listened to everything the nurse said, happily taking some of the Tylenol that she offered.

After thanking the nurse for her help, Maddie insisted on walking herself back to the truck. She made it about halfway through the office before wincing.

Muttering under his breath, Nick swore before picking Maddie up once more, carting her through the office and placing her in the truck.

"I am so sorry to ruin the day," Maddie said. "I was having a great time."

"You ruined nothing," Nick said assuredly. They drove out of the park and a small way down the road before coming upon a wooded area.

"Where are we going?" Maddie asked. "Is this the way to Inverness?"

"No," Nick said as he pulled through the winding drive. "We are going to take a little detour."

He pulled up to a log cabin with a sign in front that said "booking office." Maddie shrugged. They were going to stay in a cabin?

Nick got out of the truck and walked inside the cabin, coming out a few minutes later with a key in his hand. He got back in the truck and they drove about a mile into the woods. Nick turned down a winding driveway and they came upon a tiny little log cabin. It looked surprisingly cheery in the dark woods.

He came around the other side of the truck and once again picked Maddie up. "A girl could get used to this," Maddie said with a smile. They walked over to the red front door and Nick handed Maddie the key. She placed it in the lock and turned it in the door.

Inside, the one room cabin was adorable and thoroughly modern. A huge bed made out of logs sat on one side of the room. A small kitchenette filled one wall. Opposite of the bed was an enormous jacuzzi tub. A modern bathroom was off to the side. Maddie's eyes grew wide as she saw the view from the picture windows. They were perched on the side of a cliff, looking down at a beautiful river nestled between craggy hills. Trees dusted the hills. Maddie could imagine that there wasn't a human for miles.

Nick gently set her on the bed. Before she could say anything, he left out the front door, coming back a moment later with their bags.

"We'll take it easy and stay here for the night, okay Maddie? You need to rest your ankle."

"Are you sure?" Maddie asked. "What about your family?"

"They can wait a day," Nick insisted. "I'm going to go to the shops and pick up a few things. Do you need anything?"

Maddie shook her head, then thought about her pain. "Wait—maybe some Tylenol? I can pay you back," she insisted.

Nick smiled. "It was already on my list." He walked to the end of the bed and gently took off her other bootie. Then he walked up and fluffed the pillows behind her back. "I will be back soon."

Nick left the cabin, locking her in behind him. Maddie listened to the roar of his truck as he pulled away. After the truck faded down the drive, it was completely silent in the cabin. Maddie tried to rest, getting comfortable on the luxuriously soft bed. The only thing that she could think about, however, was that Nick was going to be sleeping next to her all night long.

The thought of Nick sleeping next to her did all types of things to Maddie. First she was excited at the thought, then nervous, then anxious. She wanted to pass out from the nerves alone. She had never spent the night with a man. The night with Calum would have been the first. She was so glad it was not.

Maddie was able to doze off soon after, desperate to get some rest before Nick came back. It was an emotional day with so much happening. With her throbbing ankle, it was hard to rest but she was exhausted.

The sound of the door opening woke Maddie up with a start. She looked over to see Nick carrying in at least five bags from the store. She watched him carry in the bags, gently setting them down in the kitchen. When he looked over at her and saw that she was awake, he let out a breath. He dug in the bags and found a box. He pulled it out. Maddie realized it was Ziploc bags. He strode over to the freezer and filled the bag with ice, then sealed it tightly.

He walked over to the bed, pulled up her wool sock, and placed the bag of ice on Maddie's ankle. Maddie was taken aback by the gentleness that he showed towards her. Nick was a natural with the alpha male protectiveness and this only solidified that for Maddie.

Nick gave her a wry smile as she got used to the cold of the ice. He stood up and walked back to the kitchen. He unloaded the bags of groceries into the fridge. Maddie spotted a bottle of wine and some meat. She would never stop being impressed with Nick's skills in the kitchen. At a first glance, he seemed like the type to live on protein shakes and box dinners. He was, however, an excellent chef. Maddie's mouth watered for the meals that he had prepared her.

Feeling a bit too much like a damsel in distress, Maddie stood up, putting weight on her ankle very gingerly. She walked to the bathroom. When she came out a few minutes later, Nick was watching her like a hawk. "If you need help, just let me know," he said, worried.

"I really appreciate it, Nick, but I think I can tinkle by myself. It's just a sprained ankle," she joked.

"I was so worried when you fell," Nick admitted as he set two wine glasses from the cupboard onto the counter. "I would never forgive myself if you got hurt under my watch,"

"Nick," Maddie said sensibly, "I'm not 'under your watch.' Come on now. I am a grown ass woman!"

"A grown arse woman who needs someone to watch out for her," Nick said as he poured the wine into the glasses.

"Wants," Maddie corrected. "A woman who *wants* someone to watch out for her. There's a difference."

"I stand corrected," Nick said, holding his hands up. "You definitely don't need anybody but yourself. I didn't mean to suggest otherwise. Rosie would kill me if she knew I made that mistake," Nick explained.

Maddie smiled, happy that Nick's sister was clearly just as headstrong as herself. Nick handed her a glass of wine and they clinked their glasses together before taking a sip.

"To Rosie," Maddie said with a smile.

"To Rosie," Nick repeated. After taking one more sip, Nick set the glass down. "Now, little one, get back into bed and elevate that foot. That's an order!"

With a smile, Maddie limped back to the bed and propped her foot on a pillow. She, surprisingly, did not mind being called "little one" by Nick. Somehow, when he said it, it was cute and not offensive at all. In fact, she kind of *liked* it.

"Have you ever dated a younger woman?" Maddie asked Nick as he began chopping vegetables.

Nick stopped cutting and glanced up at her. "Why do you ask?" he prodded.

"I was just curious," Maddie said, shrugging.

"Well, I don't really date," Nick said. "But I suppose the women I've seen have always been around my age.

"Would you ever date a woman younger than you?" she asked again.

"Would you ever date an older man?" Nick countered, setting down the knife to place his hands on the counter and stare at her pointedly.

"Yes," Maddie said. "I definitely would. Psychologists would say it's due to my unfathomable amount of daddy issues. I have to say that there's something captivating about older men. I'm not talking about like sixty-year-old men, of course, but just a little older is very intriguing." Maddie realized that she was rambling and stopped herself from continuing on. Looking over at Nick, she realized that his face was red, and he had a pained expression on his face.

Gulping, Maddie looked away and found the remote for the television. She flipped through the channels, not finding anything nearly as fascinating as the man so close to her. Nick went back to preparing the meal.

"Can I help with anything?" Maddie asked quietly.

"No," Nick replied gruffly. He took a long sip of the wine, then went on to preparing steaks. The rich aroma of sizzling meat filled the small cabin, and Maddie found herself hungry yet again, but not just for food.

Soon, Nick brought over a plate of food to the bed for Maddie. "I can get up and sit at the table," Maddie said.

"No," Nick said again. She propped the plate on her lap. Nick pulled up a chair on the other side of the bed, then kicked off his shoes and perched his feet on the bed.

They ate in silence. The glow of the television lit up the cabin. Maddie could cut the tension with a knife.

She needed to say something, anything. She couldn't just sit here in silence! If there was anything that she hated, it was the uncomfortable quiet.

"Tell me more about your family," Maddie said, finding neutral ground with talk of Nick's family.

Nick explained that Rosie was working as a teacher before she met her fiancé. Now she spent her time volunteering for charities.

Maddie thought his family sounded absolutely fantastic. She was excited to meet them and to see the people who made Nick who he is.

"Where do you see yourself in five years?" Maddie asked him as she finished off the delicious meal of steak, steamed vegetables, and buttery mashed potatoes.

Nick shrugged. "Still running the pub, maybe doing more woodworking."

"Same old, same old?" Maddie asked. "I really think you could do woodworking full time. There are websites like Etsy where you can sell your things. Is there somebody else who would take over the pub?"

"No," Nick said firmly. "The pub stays in the family. I'll run it until the day I die."

"Just because it's been in your family?" Maddie pressed. "Or because of something else?"

"It's been in the family for four generations," Nick said. "I have a sense of honor." She could tell he was getting upset with her questions.

"I understand," Maddie said, nodding.

"Do you?" He asked her. "Do you really?"

"To be honest, it doesn't seem like it's doing that well. Maybe if you tried some PR tactics, advertisements..."

"It's not about that," Nick insisted.

"Well don't you want it to succeed?" Maddie urged.

"It's doing just fine, end of discussion," Nick said. He stood up and took the plate from Maddie's hands and went to wash them in the sink.

Maddie felt terrible. Nick didn't exactly wear his feelings on his sleeve and she knew that her questions rattled him. It certainly wasn't her intention. She was just curious about his odd connection with the pub.

She stood up from the bed and walked over to where he was scrubbing a pan. She grabbed a towel from the counter and began drying the clean dishes.

"I'm sorry I pried," Maddie said sadly. "I didn't mean to be so nosy."

"No, I'm the one who is sorry," Nick said. "I shouldn't have reacted like that. You were just asking questions. It's just not something that I'm ready to talk about."

"I get that," Maddie said as she reached to put some plates in the cupboard.

"Thanks for understanding," he said as he handed her the last of the silverware. After tucking it in a drawer, Maddie turned towards the rest of the cabin, leaning up against the counter.

"It's quite the cabin, isn't it?" She said. "That tub looks amazing."

"Would you like to take a soak?" he asked her. Maddie blushed as she thought about being naked in the tub with Nick there.

"It's not exactly private," she said.

"It's just us," Nick said, turning towards Maddie. He placed his hands, which were still damp and full of the citrusy dish soap scent, on her shoulders. "Plus, I saw some bubble bath over there. I won't be able to see anything anyway."

"It wouldn't be awkward?" Maddie asked him reluctantly.

"Nah," Nick said, leading her over to the bed. He had her sit on the end of the bed. Falling to his knees, he pulled her socks off gently. With quick movements, he unwrapped the bandage from her ankle, carefully rolling it up to be ready for later.

"You don't have to do this," Maddie insisted. Nick looked up from the ground, his dark blue eyes simmering. "It's my pleasure," he said.

Maddie gulped as he stood up, then held his hands out for hers. They walked over to the tub. Nick leaned over and turned the faucet on, checking the temperature with his hand. He poured the pink bubble bath into the tub and the fruity scent of peaches and strawberries filled the room.

"How are we going to do this now?" Maddie asked.

"I'll turn around while you get undressed," Nick said. "I just don't want you to hurt yourself getting in."

"I'll be careful," Maddie assured him.

"Then it's settled. Let me know when you're ready," Nick said as he walked over to the window, gazing at the sunset as the wind picked up outside, shaking the trees something fierce.

Hurriedly, Maddie completely undressed, sliding off her shirt and bra and her tight jeans and panties. She sat on the edge of the tub, testing the water with her toes. It was the perfect temperature. She slid into the water, her body instantly covered up with hundreds of bubbles. With a sigh, she looked towards Nick, who stood tall in front of the window, his back sternly straight.

"I'm covered," Maddie said, her voice unexpectedly gravelly.

Nick swiveled around, his eyes growing hooded when he took in the sight. Maddie's blonde hair was swept into a messy bun, the bubbles going up to her neck in the big tub. Her pink-painted toes poked out of the jacuzzi.

When Maddie saw the way that Nick looked at her, as if he wanted to both protect and ravish her, Maddie's heart sped up. She could have never predicted that any of this would happen, even in her wildest dreams.

Thoughts of dreams went out the window when Nick took a step closer to her and began to unbutton his shirt, one delectable button at a time.

Biting her lip, Maddie watched fascinated to see what he would do next. She had a feeling she wouldn't mind whatever his next move was.

Chapter 11

Maddie gulped as Nick continued to unbutton his flannel shirt. "What are you doing?" she asked him, trying to sound casual, as if hot men stripped in front of her all the time.

She tried not to let her disappointment show as he removed his flannel shirt to see a black undershirt."It's getting warm in here with all this steam from your bath," Nick said, not taking his eyes off of her as he tossed his shirt on the back of a chair.

Maddie nodded. "You know, you can take more off if you'd like," she said teasingly.

"Oh is that so?" he replied, smiling. "I might just take you up on that," he said, reaching for his pants. Her eyes must have widened to the size of saucers because Nick pulled his hand up and started laughing. "I'm just teasing you, Maddie," he said with a wink.

"You're so mean to me," Maddie smiled.

"You don't really want to see me naked, do you?" he asked.

"I mean, we are just friends," Maddie said. "Right?" After she said it, Maddie wasn't sure whether that meant they should or should not see each other naked.

"Right," Nick agreed. He walked over to the counter and refilled their wine glasses, then set one on the edge of the tub for Maddie. He sat on the bed in front of her as she reached for the glass and took the world's biggest sip.

"How's the bath?" He asked her.

"Luxurious," she said, settling back in and relaxing. "Do you want to go next?"

"Nah," Nick said. "I'm not much of a bath man."

"But you would actually fit in this tub!" Maddie said.

"That's true, isn't it?" he pondered. "It could fit two of me."

"Definitely," Maddie said, stretching out. They settled into the comfortable silence that she was used to with Nick. He walked over to a gas-powered fireplace and flipped it on. Soon there was a roaring fire in the room. With darkness settling in outside, she could only see Nick's features from the light of the fire.

The water eventually began to cool off. After feeling relaxed and clean from the bath, Maddie broke their silence. "I'm done now," she said quietly.

Nick stood up and grabbed an oversized towel from one of the shelves."Be careful standing up," he ordered.

"I will," Maddie said. Nick unfolded the towel and held it outstretched in front of him, turning his head away. Maddie stood up and carefully made her way out of the tub and wrapped the towel around her body. She could feel the heat coming from Nick's body as she stood close to him. Clutching the towel behind her, Maddie patted her body dry. The cabin was silent except for the water draining from the tub.

She walked over to the suitcase and carefully bent down to get out a pair of leggings and a t-shirt. She moved to walk into the bathroom to change.

"Wait," Nick said. She turned around and found him standing in front of the bed, his chest heaving up and down. "Let me wrap your foot before you walk any further," he said, holding up the wrap.

Maddie nodded and walked towards the bed , sitting down on the end just as before. Nick kneeled in front of her and Maddie felt self-conscious. No man had ever been so close to her naked body before. She was nervous to have him so close to her. Would he see that she hadn't shaved her legs in a few days? What about that scar on her thigh from when she fell out of a tree when she was six?

Nick carefully wrapped her ankle, placing the clips on gently. He was so close to her. Maddie's skin was still damp from the tub. She clutched the towel harder, struggling to keep her cool.

"Tell me you feel this too," Maddie said deeply. "Tell me it's not just me having another silly crush."

Nick looked up at Maddie. "I feel it," he said. "I've never felt anything like this before," he admitted.

"Me neither, obviously," Maddie said with a nervous laugh. "It's not like I've been with a guy before," she explained.

At that, Nick's eyes darkened before she knew it."I don't know how much longer I can resist you," Nick said firmly.

"So don't," Maddie said.

Nick looked up at her incredulously, as if he could hardly believe this was really happening.

"Really?" He asked her. "Are you sure?"

"I've never been so sure of anything in my life," she said.

Slowly, gently, Nick leaned down and kissed Maddie's injured ankle. It was the biggest turn on in her life to see such a massive, authoritative man on his knees in front of her. He began to kiss up her legs, eventually reaching her thighs.

Maddie realized she was holding her breath. Exhaling, she reached out and grabbed Nick's shirt in the middle. Pulling him up onto the bed, he climbed on top of her. Maddie's head hit the pillows as she fell backwards. Nothing had ever felt as good as this, she realized.

Nick's weight on top of her felt luxuriously sexy. As he leaned over her, his face came so close to hers that she thought she would faint. Before he kissed her, Maddie felt his beard scratching her face, his whiskers teasing her skin. She realized that she had dreamed about what his beard felt like. As much as she didn't want to admit it to herself, she was over the moon for Nicholas O'Shaughnessy.

With a free hand, Nick gently clutched Maddie's chin. "Madeline Danzer, you captivate me," he said, before plunging his mouth towards hers and kissing her with both power and seduction.

When he eventually broke the kiss, Maddie managed to sigh and say, "The feeling is mutual." With a smile, Nick went back to kissing her, both gently and firmly. He broke it to plant kisses on her neck, licking various spots only to gently bite them before nursing them with a kiss.

With a moan, Maddie threw her head back. She had never felt this way before, and was not certain she would ever feel such eroticism again.

"Touch me," Maddie begged. "Please." Her whole body was tense and hot, craving for his touch.

"Yes, Maddie," Nick said. Sitting up, he straddled Maddie's waist as he stripped his shirt off. Maddie could hardly believe his body. With his shirt off, she was able to see the full extent of his tattoos. Even in just the firelight, she could hardly believe her eyes as the dark ink was like a maze over his arms and torso. Dozens of designs highlighted his taut muscles. Light freckles poked out from his chest hair.

With a smile, Maddie leaned forward and gently pushed Nick off of her. Turning the tables, she climbed on top of him, her legs stretched wide by his big body. She could feel the hard outline of his cock through his jeans. Maddie let the towel fall off of her, now gloriously naked in the firelight.

With a sharp inhale, Nick gazed up at Maddie's body. "Oh Maddie, love," Nick said. He stretched his arms to her hips, pulling them closer to him. With a firm hand, he gently smacked her bottom. Maddie squealed as she leaned into him, laughing.

She kissed him playfully, enjoying being in charge.

"You're a naughty girl," he said quietly, his accent heavy as he rolled his r's.

"You're a terrible influence," Maddie said as she sat up once again, grinding into his cock. She wasn't an expert, but it felt enormous and hard as steel.

With a moan, Nick reached up to touch Maddie's breasts, cupping them lovingly before leaning forward to nip on one, then the other. Maddie nearly screamed at the sensation, never feeling anything like it before.

As she sat perched on top of him, Nick continued to lean forward to suck on her nipples, tenderly rubbing her breasts.

The more that Nick used his mouth on her, the more aroused she became. Maddie could feel her clitoris tingling, desperate to be touched. She continued to grind on his cock.

"Take your pants off," Maddie begged, needing to be closer to Nick and his cock and past his chest. With one fell swoop, Nick unbuckled his pants and kicked them. His cock bobbed up in front of Maddie, standing rock hard and at attention.

Maddie gripped Nick's cock gently at first, not entirely sure what to do with it but feeling confident enough in her research to try it. Nick's eyes roamed her face, desperate to gauge a reaction. Her small hand wrapped around his hard shaft, and she began to move it up and down. Nick stifled a groan as she touched him, teasing him with each of her fingers.

Suddenly and without warning, Nick hooked his fingers underneath Maddie's armpits and hauled her forward, over his cock. With her legs spread, he settled her pussy over his head.

"Hold onto the headboard," he murmured underneath her. Maddie held onto the slats of the headboard fervently as Nick began to move his lips underneath her, kissing her pussy with rough, needy movements.

Maddie moaned loudly as Nick licked her, his tongue alternating between swirling around her pussy and teasing her clitoris. "God!" she screamed as Nick began building her up for an orgasm. She was ready to burst at any moment. With one more swirl of his tongue, Maddie came apart above him, grinding her pussy into his face as she gripped the headboard. Her knees fell on each side of his head as she continued to come, never wanting the feeling to end. She moaned Nick's name over and over as she came, her fervent cries letting him know she needed more.

Nick grabbed her ass and smacked both cheeks once more, then began feasting on her again. His strong tongue swirled up and down her pussy, taking in all of her juices. There was nothing that he wanted more than this.

Teasing her clit again, Nick began winding up the little bud once more. Maddie could feel how soaked her pussy was as she sat on his face. His tongue lapped up all of her juices and Maddie prepared to come once more. Gripping tightly to the wooden headboard, Maddie bounced up and down on his face, his tongue darting in and out of her pussy. The buildup was quicker this time, and more furtive as she released.

"Oh God, Nick," she murmured. "Give it to me," she begged. Everything was in slow motion as she came again. His tongue began to move dangerously slow, taking its time darting around her clit. With a groan of need, she released once more.

Catching her breath, Maddie sighed as she fell next to Nick on the bed. She looked over at him, smiling and wiping his beard on the sheets. Biting her bottom lip with her teeth, Maddie groaned as she leaned over and kissed him, tasting her own juices on his lips.

"Thank you for that," Maddie said. "It was amazing."

"I'm glad you liked it," he said with a grin.

"Now it's my turn to make you come," Maddie said assertively, sitting up to gaze at his hard cock.

Nick's eyes grew wide at the idea. "You don't have to if you don't want to, Maddie," he said quietly.

"Oh but I do," Maddie replied. Reaching out to grab his cock, Maddie smiled as it stood even more at attention. With both hands, she worked them up and down his shaft.

Maddie could hear Nick's heavy breathing as she stroked his cock. Taking a chance, she reached down and gently cupped his balls. He groaned heavily and thrust forward when she did this. Taking that as a sign to continue, Maddie kept it up, massaging his balls and working his shaft.

Kneeling next to him, Maddie leaned down and gently kissed the tip of his cock. She could hear Nick cursing under his breath as she took his cock in her mouth, licking it and swirling her tongue around the big head of his cock. He gently grabbed her hair, moaning as she continued to push his cock further into her mouth.

She began to bob her mouth up and down his shaft, enjoying hearing the pleasurable noises that Nick made as she continued working his cock. As she moved her way down his cock, Maddie tongued Nick's balls, then slid her lips all the way up again. She continued this until Nick muttered her name. "I'm not going to last," he choked out.

Instead of pulling up like he expected her to, Maddie pushed her mouth down further on his cock until Nick exploded, coming over and over as his cock thrust uncontrollably into her mouth. When she was certain that he was done, Maddie swallowed his essence and then sat back up, licking her lips.

Nick pulled her towards him on the bed, enveloping her in his arms. Maddie's heart was beating fast and was convinced that he could feel it upon his chest. That was, quite certainly, the most scandalous thing that Maddie had ever done! Before she was able to overthink it, Nick touched her cheek, then leaned over to gently catch her lips with his. The two soon passed out in the big bed, the warmth of the fire keeping them cozy throughout the night.

Returning His Love

Chapter 12

Maddie woke up to a warm body next to her. She leaned into it some more as she felt a big arm wrap around her. It was entirely possible, she mused, that they did not move the entire night. She felt entirely safe in his arms. Her heart began to race as she thought about everything that happened last night. Nick was the first man to ever make her come, and he did so in such an unconventional and sexy way that she wanted to scream just thinking about it.

Just when she thought that they hadn't moved, Maddie realized that another bag of ice was perched on her ankle, the ice relatively fresh. She looked up at Nick's sleeping face and smiled at the considerate gesture.

She could not beat the feeling of joy that things on this trip turned out okay, even after all the stuff with

Calum. Even though Nick was not the type of guy that she usually found doing a double take for, there was something about his soul that captivated her. She wanted to make him smile and, she mused, to make him come.

Moving an arm under the blankets, Maddie reached down and grabbed Nick's cock, which was still hard. With a groan, he leaned into her hand and began to thrust. As he woke up fully, Nick moaned as he continued to thrust. Then, pulling away, he pushed himself up onto his arms and threw back the covers. One hand slipped under the sheets and he found Maddie's pussy.

She was already soaked when his fingers began exploring her. As he circled her clit with his rough fingers, Maddie squirmed and begged for him not to stop. Nick moved his fingers down towards her pussy and began to trace shapes around her sensitive opening. Slowly, he pressed one finger into her, eventually moving it in and out as gently as he could. Maddie could feel an orgasm building up inside her. With his thumb, Nick circled her clit as he fucked Maddie's pussy with his fingers, wanting her to come all over his hand.

Maddie arched her back as the orgasm began building up, Nick's fingers moving deftly in and out of her. She was never wetter than at this moment, with Nick using everything in his power to bring her pleasure. The orgasm overtook her entire body, making her shiver from head to toe. Nick's thrusting slowed as he let it pulse through her. Gently, he pulled his fingers out of her and wrapped his arms around her.

They stayed that way for some time, until Maddie reluctantly realized that they should get up. "I need to shower," she said. "And then I'll make you breakfast."

"Deal," Nick said, getting up out of bed and sliding his jeans on. He went into the kitchen to start coffee as Maddie went and took a quick shower. By the time she came out, a piping hot cup waited for her on the counter. Nick had made the bed and was standing at the window, looking at the view.

Maddie smiled at him as she packed her suitcase, suddenly shy around the man who she was so intimate with just minutes before. Nick silently went into the bathroom and she heard the shower start. Sitting at the breakfast bar, Maddie remarked at how much better her ankle felt this morning. She leaned down to wrap it up once more, then nursed a cup of coffee as she watched the river flow below her.

A few minutes later, Nick came from the bathroom and put their bags near the door.

"I was going to make you breakfast," Maddie said, "But I didn't have anything to make you."

Nick laughed. "That's okay. We will pick something up on the way out of town. How's the ankle?" he asked as he walked towards her. He ran his hands up and down her arms and pulled her into him gently. Maddie smiled as she fell into his embrace.

"I feel a hundred times better," Maddie said. "The early morning ice helped quite a bit," she continued. "Thank you for that."

"Anytime, Maddie," Nick said genuinely.

"If you're not careful, " Maddie warned, "I'm going to catch feelings for you."

"The feeling is mutual," Nick replied. They looked good together today. Maddie was wearing a light pink sweater and a pair of gray leggings. Nick was wearing a purple flannel shirt and his trusty jeans.

"I'm excited to meet your family," Maddie said as she cleaned up the coffee and tidied up the kitchen.

"It will be fun," Nick said. Maddie could have sworn that she caught a hint of nervousness in his voice, but brushed it off.

He carried their bags to the truck, then came back to make sure Maddie was able to get into the truck before locking up. He climbed into the truck. Maddie pulled her phone out of her bag for the first time since yesterday to snap a photo of the cabin and was taken aback from the many missed video calls from Melissa and emails.

"Who is that guy who is KISSING you in front of the castle?" She wrote. "That doesn't look like Calum." *Oh shit.* Maddie's heart raced as she looked back at her last email and realized that she had accidentally sent her sister the picture of Nick planting a kiss on her cheek along with the rest of the castle pictures.

Instead of replying, Maddie shut off her phone and tucked it back in her bag.

"Everything okay?" Nick asked.

"Yeah, just catching up on emails," Maddie said with a smile.

They went to a drive-through to get more coffee and some quick breakfast, then were on their way to Inverness. It was only an hour's drive to the city and Maddie was nervous to meet everyone. She was especially nervous to meet Rosie, who Nick held in such high regard.

As they drove along, Maddie found herself stealing more and more glances at Nick. It was hard to believe that she was so intimate with *Nick*, her only friend in Scotland. Out of all the men, she never thought he would be the one to introduce her to the world of sex. Secretly, she hoped last night wouldn't be the last time they were together.

The more she was around Nick, the more she realized how truly attractive he was. While she first just saw him as a gentle giant, she now found him to be really sexy, with his big beard and body covered in tattoos. It turned her on to know what he looked like without his clothes on, and blushed a bit to think that he knew what she looked like naked, too.

Her nerves caught up with her the closer they came. "What's the plan?" Maddie asked Nick as he exited the highway.

"We will stop by Oliver and Rosie's to drop off these things and see the family. Then, I believe they want to go over to the wedding venue and do some setting up."

"Sounds great," Maddie said. Maddie noticed they travelled further and further from the highway. Nick pulled down a narrow gravel road and they came upon an enormous gated country estate. Maddie gasped as she looked at the huge white house—if it could be called that. He typed in a code and the gate opened. Nick pulled up the truck and parked it in front of the house. Maddie stepped out and began to look around. The home was enormous, with two tall stories and rows and rows of windows. She had never seen anything like it in the States.

The front door opened and a short brunette ran out and into Nick's arms. "Nicky!" she shouted. He laughed and hugged her, lifting her up as he did.

"How are you, Rosie?" he asked her as he laughed.

"Just great, even better now that you're here." Maddie couldn't help but smile at the sibling reunion. It made her think of Melissa. She felt guilty for not responding to her. It felt silly, but she wasn't ready to share Nick with anybody yet, even if she was just telling people that they were friends.

Maddie came out of her thoughts to find Rosie staring at her, smiling. "And who is this, Nick?" Rosie asked as she walked up to Maddie.

"Rosie, this is Maddie. She's from the States, and I invited her to tag along for the scenery," Nick explained.

"Aww, well it's so nice to meet you, Maddie," Rosie said, linking arms with her and leading her inside. "Now you must come in and meet everyone!" Maddie looked back at Nick who was carrying their bags inside and smiled. He looked nervous at the two of them together, but followed them inside anyway.

Maddie was captivated at once with the beautiful mansion. While the interior was expansive, it was so cozy that she almost thought that she was at home in her own living room. Rosie led Maddie into the sitting room and she sat in a huge oversize leather couch.

"Would you like a spot of tea?" Rosie asked Maddie as she poured two cups.

Maddie nodded and Rosie handed her one of the cups. Looking around, Maddie saw dozens of family pictures hanging on the walls. She smiled as she thought about all of the pictures that Melissa collected back at their old apartment.

A gaggle of voices and heavy Scottish accents tore Maddie away from her observations. Rosie stood up when Nick walked in with a handsome blonde man, who looked exceptionally petite next to him, and a beautiful middle-aged brunette who appeared to be the spitting image of Rosie except a few decades older.

"Mum, this is Nick's friend, Maddie," Rosie said when the woman spotted Maddie.

"Ohh!" The woman said as she came dodging over to Maddie, who quickly set down her teacup and stood up. The woman scooped Maddie up in a big bearhug and squeezed tightly. "I'm Doreen," she said. "Nick's mum."

Maddie hadn't felt that kind of motherly hug in some time, and she was shocked at how much emotion she felt over it.

"My Nicholas told me to expect you," she said as she pulled away. "We are so happy to have you here."

Maddie looked stunned as she looked from Nick's mother back to Nick, then to Rosie and back again. Nick told them about her? What did it mean?

Nick stood in the corner next to the man, blushing furiously as he sipped his tea. He refused to make eye contact with Maddie.

"Thank you so much for having me," Maddie said, clearing her throat.

"Of course!" Doreen stepped back from Maddie and sat down next to her. She grabbed Maddie's hand and patted it. "Now tell me about yourself. Tell me everything. Tell me about your family. Mum and Dad, brothers and sisters..." she began.

Nick stepped out from his spot in the corner of the room and this and said, "Mum, don't—."

"It's okay," Maddie said calmly to Nick. "I'd be happy to tell you all about them, Doreen," Maddie began. "Unfortunately, my parents are no longer with us. However, I am very close to my older sister, Melissa. I would reckon to bet that she and I might be just as close as Nick and Rosie."

"Oh, sweetie," Doreen said quietly, clutching Maddie's hand. "I am so sorry about your parents. You must know what it's like then." Maddie was confused at this comment but didn't get a chance to ask what she meant before another figure entered the room.

Everyone looked over to the door to see a man, who was as enormous and bearded as Nick, wheeling himself in on a wheelchair. He caught eyes with Maddie and she couldn't mistake the same glimmer in his eyes that were in Nick's.

"Honey, this is Nick's friend, Maddie. She's from the States," Doreen began. "Maddie, this is Nick and Rosie's father, Elliot. And where are my manners?" Doreen continued. "This handsome lad over here is Rosie's betrothed, Oliver."

Maddie stood up quickly from the couch and walked over to the two men. "It's so nice to meet both of you," Maddie said as she extended her hand first to Elliot, who caught her hand firmly, and then to Oliver. "Thank you so much for having me in your home," Maddie continued. "It has been so nice to get to see Scotland with Nick."

Nick's father looked up at his son and gave him a nod, as if he approved of Maddie, and then turned back to Maddie and flashed a smile, which was dangerously similar to Nick's. "I see where Nick gets his build from," Maddie said with a laugh.

"Well it's certainly not from me!" Doreen said with a laugh as she stood next to Nick, barely coming up to his shoulders.

Soon after, Rosie brought Nick and Maddie up the grand staircase and down the hall as Nick carried their bags. Maddie found herself limping a bit and reminded herself to take some of the Tylenol that Nick bought her yesterday.

She pointed to one door and Nick slipped inside, handing Maddie's bag to Rosie. Rosie opened the door next to Nick's and Maddie followed her. Inside, she found the most exquisite guest room that she had ever seen.

With pale pink walls, the bedroom was entirely feminine. A delicate cherry vanity set matched the four-poster bed.

"This is beautiful," Maddie said in awe as she explored the room.

"Nick made the furniture, you know," Rosie said proudly as she swept a hand over the armoire.

"He's so freaking talented," Maddie said as she noticed the detailing that went into the woodwork.

"That he is," Rosie said proudly. "Well, I'll let you get settled. There is a bathroom to yourself. If you need anything, you just let me know, okay? Oliver and I are so happy to have you. We are going over to the venue in an hour or so, and we'd love for you to join us."

"Oh absolutely," Maddie said, her blonde hair bobbing as she nodded. "I'd love to come. Thank you,"

"Of course," Rosie said, smiling as she shut the door the bedroom and left Maddie alone.

After touching up her makeup and freshening up in the bathroom, Maddie walked into the bedroom and peered out the window. She saw stables and Oliver outside riding one of the horses, a beautiful black stallion, and gasped. The horses were gorgeous. She should have known there would be horses!

After watching for a few more minutes, a knock on the bedroom door startled her. Maddie strode over to the door, and opened it, finding Nick standing there, a smile on his face.

"Hi," she said to him, suddenly shy.

"Maddie," Nick said. She saw the need in his eyes and had the immense urge to kiss him. Grabbing him by the middle of his flannel shirt, Maddie pulled him into the room and shut the door.

"I've been waiting to do this for hours," Maddie said breathlessly. Gently pushing his back against the closed door, Nick smiled as he let her take charge.

"I've been waiting for you to do this forever," Nick said.

Closing the distance between them, she stood up on her tip toes and kissed Nick firmly. Wrapping her arms around his neck, she leaned in, lengthening the kiss, deepening it.

His lips felt so soft against hers that she could have sworn that he moisturized them. The bushy beard scratched at her neck as she continued the kiss, and she relished in that feeling. Slowly, his tongue reached out to dance with hers.

There was something so fascinating about Nick. How long had she actually been attracted to him before admitting it to herself? Had it always been there?

Nick moaned as Maddie gently nipped at his bottom lip. He caught her ass and gave it a quick slap. She smiled, knowing that he could not possibly relinquish control for much longer.

Scooping down, Nick picked her up and clutched her tightly. She giggled as he lifted her effortlessly. Taking his face in her hands, Maddie smiled before giving him a long kiss. She could feel his erection as it grazed her sex, poking into her each time she moved.

Maddie could feel a smile forming on Nick's mouth before he moved to throw her down on the bed. Before he could make it the entire way to the bed, they were interrupted by Nick's mothers voice screeching up the stairs to them. "Get on down here, you two! I made lunch for you!"

Maddie bit her lip to try to stifle a laugh. Nick groaned, then threw her down on the bed anyway. She stifled a yelp and then went to stand up to follow him downstairs.

As they made their way down the stairs, Nick reached out to squeeze Maddie's hand. Was it possible for her heart to implode from this gesture? She could have sworn that her heart had not ever beat faster than in that moment.

The kitchen looked as if it belonged in a five star restaurant. Nick's Mom was scooping up bowls of soup. Doreen turned as the two walked in and smiled and them. "It's so nice to see a smile on Nick's face," she said proudly.

Maddie looked up at Nick, who was blushing again. "Come on, Mum," Nick begged as he grabbed a plate with a sandwich on it and sat down at the breakfast bar.

"Well, can't a mother observe these things?" she asked, setting a bowl of soup and a plate with a sandwich in the spot next to Nick. "Sit here, honey, and eat up. Is Nick feeding you well enough?" Doreen chastised. Maddie smiled, thinking about the disgusting amount of food that Nick made or bought for Maddie on a regular basis.

"Yeah, Nick," Maddie teased. "You ever think about feeding me every once in a while?"

Nick grunted as he bit into the sandwich. The entire family made their way in, Oliver still in his riding gear. She got the chance to observe Rosie. While she was very petite, she was definitely curvy, just like Doreen. She seemed like the type of person that Maddie would like to be friends with, and for that Maddie was grateful.

The three men in the room groaned when Maddie asked the women to tell her more about the wedding, and Doreen and Rosie went into lavish detail about the ceremony and the reception, talking over each other and getting into a short-lived argument about whether the priest was bald or just graying.

If there was one thing that Maddie enjoyed more than baby showers, it was weddings. While she was a sucker for the games at baby showers and the joy of a new person coming into the world, weddings were the ultimate in her book. What could be more romantic than a wedding? Nothing, she decided.

After finishing lunch, Maddie insisted on helping clean up the dishes. Nick and Oliver went outside to begin unloading his truck. She could tell that Rosie and Doreen were eager to ask her dozens of nosy questions but were much too polite to do so.

Doing what Maddie did best, she told them all about her life back home as a librarian and bragged about her sister and Jakob. Thinking about them made Maddie feel guilty all over again for ignoring her sister. What was this weird behavior? It wasn't like her at all to ignore her sister, especially about something as silly as a guy.

Maddie realized that she was ashamed that things with Calum did not work out. She already felt guilty about being so secretive about her trip here that she did not want to make it seem like she was a complete and total failure. The picture with Nick just solidified that everything basically went to shit, but she was at least happy about what came from it.

She knew that Melissa put a lot of pressure on herself to make sure that everything in Maddie's life was good. She went to great lengths to protect her from the world. After everything that happened with her parents, Melissa quickly became her parental figure even though she was just a few years older. Melissa worked a crazy amount of jobs to make sure that Maddie could get the prom dress she wanted, had time to study, and had appointments with the best therapist in greater Chicagoland.

Maddie knew that Melissa deserved more from her, which is why she resolved to call her that night and explain everything that was going on, or at least part of it.

Maddie once more got in Nick's truck as they made their way to the wedding venue. She noticed that Doreen had a special van so that Elliot could just go straight in the back without leaving his wheelchair.

Oliver and Rosie rode in a Rolls Royce, and Maddie was only momentarily shocked at their vehicle.

After they left the estate, they only drove for ten minutes or so before Maddie noticed a large castle in the distance. "Wow, look at that beautiful castle!" Maddie said, peering out the window. "Can you imagine what it looks like inside?" she asked.

Nick turned to her and said, "Well, yes, actually. That's where Rosie and Oliver are getting married." He slowed the truck before the castle, then turned into the property. He parked in front of it. Two large trucks were parked outside and workers unloaded chairs and tables.

"You've got to be shitting me!" Maddie said incredulously. "This is going to be one spectacular wedding," she furthered.

"I don't think Rosie and Mum would have it any other way," he said.

Maddie watched as Doreen and Oliver pulled up. Once they all got out, Maddie stood in awe of the castle. It was a light brown palace with dozens fo turrets and windows. She stood fascinated as she saw an observation tower. She decided that she could stare at the castle for hours.

"What is this place?" She asked Rosie incredulously. The rolling hills behind the estate were covered in hundreds of trees, nestling the castle in a cozy enclave.

"It's the Aldourie Castle Estate," Rosie said, coming up next to Maddie. "It was built in 1625. One of Ollie's distant relatives was the first to live here. It's been a big part of his family ever since. We rented out the entire place for the wedding. It's the place to be on Loch Ness."

Maddie's ears perked up. "Loch Ness? As in, Nessie? Where?"

Rosie laughed and pointed to the body of water a distance away from the castle. "There it is," she said.

"No freakin' way!" Maddie said excitedly, squinting her eyes in hopes of spotting the Loch Ness Monster.

"If you're looking for monsters, love, you'll be looking a long time," Nick said. Maddie pursed her lips at him and took one more glance at the lake before turning to Rosie and walking inside.

"Non-believer," she mumbled at Nick.

Maddie quickly forgot about the lake when she walked in the castle. If she thought the castle that they toured before was exquisite, this took it to an entirely new level.

The rooms were all decorated meticulously. She felt as if she was on the set of some period drama as she walked through. The detailed wallpaper and deep reds and blues of the paint was almost too much. Portraits of people long gone decorated the walls, with grand chandeliers in every room.

Maddie nearly fainted when she wandered into one of the many libraries. Shelves and shelves of books plastered the walls, with dozens of chairs and couches to sit on. She could imagine curling up with one of the books and enjoying it in front of a fire.

The tour continued on. Maddie watched Rosie and Doreen argue about the floral arrangements at the head of the grand ballroom, smiling when the two came to an agreement and then hugged each other, apologizing for bickering.

She spotted Nick and his father outside, Nick pushing his father's wheelchair as the two talked. Oliver was deep in conversation with the castle director. Maddie took a moment to take it all in, then went over to Doreen and Rosie.

They spent the afternoon planning out the decorations for the ceremony. Maddie noticed that Rosie and Doreen tried to include her, asking her opinion on centerpieces and more. She enjoyed being able to participate in the celebration, and wished that she would be able to see it all come together.

Smiling to herself, Maddie reckoned that this was the most fun that she had in a long time, and she reminded herself to relish the moment. She could *definitely* get used to this.

Chapter 13

The rest of the day went by quickly. Maddie easily became friends with Rosie and enjoyed watching Doreen and Rosie interact. The two were more like sisters than anything else, constantly bickering about unimportant things and then making up right away. While it was hard to not feel more than a little jealous of their relationship, she kept thinking about Melissa and was glad to have her.

After finishing up at the castle, they all decided to go out to dinner together. Maddie quickly discovered that Oliver was a successful restauranteur, owning a few different restaurants in Inverness. Maddie couldn't be more thrilled at the thought, and was especially tickled when she found out that he owned a pizza place.

They settled on his steakhouse for dinner, and as they crowded into the restaurant and sat at a large table,

Returning His Love

Maddie never felt so comfortable in her life. Rosie was absolutely hilarious and she treasured hearing funny stories about her teaching career. As a librarian, Maddie could relate to a lot of them. She found herself missing the library. She pulled out her phone to show everyone pictures of her little public library. Nick was enthralled when she spoke, hanging on to every word.

When she went to slip her phone back into her bag, Nick caught her hand under the table, giving it a squeeze. She looked up at him and smiled, then leaned in and bumped his shoulder with hers. The table quieted and Maddie looked up to see everyone looking at her and Nick. She tried not to take it too personally when Nick unwrapped his hand from hers, setting it on his own lap.

Maddie knew that Nick was not really the type to be into public displays of affection, so she understood why he was embarrassed. Instead of focusing on it, Maddie asked everyone to share the rest of the plans for the wedding preparation.

When they got back to the house, everyone was pretty tired. She was excited to meet Nick's aunt, who was arriving the next day. Rosie said that she was a hilarious woman.

After changing into her pajamas, Maddie walked over to Nick's room and knocked on the door. A few moments later, the door opened. Nick was wearing a black undershirt and his jeans.

"Hi," she said, smiling softly.

"Hello, Maddie," Nick said gently, opening the door wider, inviting him in. She loved how his eyes darkened when he said her name, his long eyelashes hooding his eyes.

160

Nick's room was painted a dark blue, with similar furniture. "Rosie said you made the furniture in my bedroom. Did you make this too?" she asked, touching one of the spindles on the four poster bed.

"Yes," Nick said, walking over to the bed and sitting down on it.

"It's beautiful, Nick. Just gorgeous," Maddie said seriously.

"Thank you," he murmured. Nick patted the bed next to him and Maddie sat down next to him, nestling in under his arm. "What do you think of everyone?" he asked her, sounding a bit nervous.

"Your family is just lovely," Maddie said. "Your Mom is so sweet, Rosie is the best, and your Dad seems so nice," she said.

Nick nodded. "Dad's always been a quiet one. Ever since he turned sixty he's been in the chair. Doctors say it's just years of hard work that led him to it. He does well with it, given everything."

"He looks so much like you," Maddie said, getting even closer to Nick as they laid on the bed, both looking up towards the ceiling.

Nick's woodsy scent emanated off of him. Maddie tried to not look like a creeper as she leaned in a bit further to take a deep inhale.

"People say that a lot," Nick said.

"I have to message my sister," Maddie said suddenly, realizing that she really needed to bite the bullet. "I better go do that before I get too sleepy."

"Okay, love, you do that," Nick said, sitting up to let Maddie go.

"I guess I'll see you tomorrow?" Maddie said as she approached the door.

"Definitely," Nick said, smiling.

"Until tomorrow, then," Maddie said, leaving the room and walking over to her own.

She sat on the bed and starting writing a email to her sister. Instead of telling her the truth, she laughed it off and said that Nick was just her tour guide and being silly. She said nothing about Calum, but promised her that things were going well and that she was having the time of her life.

When she finished writing the email, she sent it without giving herself a chance to change her mind. She turned off her phone and realized that she was more exhausted than she initially thought. After turning off the light, Maddie fell fast asleep.

It wasn't until she heard voices in the hallway that Maddie stirred from her deep sleep. As she opened her eyes, bright sunshine hit her. Pulling the covers up over her head, Maddie listened to the voices. It appeared to be Nick talking to someone in a hushed tone.

"We are *just* friends," he insisted curtly.

"Sure you are," Rosie said sarcastically. "We can all see the writing on the wall. I don't know why you are trying to hide it."

"There's nothing to hide," Nick said. "It's not serious. There's nothing happening," he furthered. "She's a young girl from the States. Nothing is going to happen," he said. Maddie could hardly hide her disappointment as she listened, not daring to move an inch.

"Sure, fine, whatever. I want her at the wedding," Rosie insisted.

"It's not a good idea," Nick said curtly. "I was going to drive her back before the weekend. She has other things to do."

"It's my wedding," Rosie said. "And if I want the pretty American to be there, she will be there." She could hear Rosie's footsteps departing and Nick's door closing. Once she was certain that nobody was in the hallway, she got up from the bed and went into the bathroom.

Just friends. Just a young girl from the States. Is that really what Nick thought of her? Maddie knew she had a penchant for being naive, but were they truly only *just friends*? What was with the change of heart? Why did Nick insist on being so wishy washy? She hardly thought that their activities in the cabin were friendly activities, but maybe that was her being ignorant.

Groaning as she brushed her teeth, Maddie stepped into the shower and allowed herself to pretend that she wasn't in an entirely uncomfortable situation. She could hardly believe that Nick would say such things, especially when he was so damn kind towards her. It infuriated her to no end. She felt just as she did when Calum blew her off and downplayed what they had.

Maybe she was certifiable, Maddie deducted. That was the only reasonable explanation for so many men seemingly thinking that they were just friends when Maddie clearly thought they were so much more. Maybe all of the books that she read and romances she watched were full of lies. Cary Grant wasn't really going to come along and profess his love to her, was he? No, she mused, Cary Grant was going to come along and play with her heart and then insist on remaining just friends. She shook the thought from her head.

"Cary Grant would never do that me!" she said aloud in the shower as she rinsed the shampoo from her hair.

It was reasons like this, other than just being way too honest and generally considered a friend and only a friend by men, that Maddie was still single. She knew that men like her sister's Jakob were one in a million, and so desperately wanted to find one of her own. However, it appeared that Nick was just like the rest of them.

Maddie took her time doing her makeup, brushing on a deep red lipstick to match her sweater. If Nick wanted to be just friends, fine. She started out being friends with him and things were perfectly fine. Their evening in the cabin was just a fluke. No problem. Maddie enjoyed herself and she knew he did, too.

Slipping her boots on, she walked out of her room and down the stairs. Everyone was in the kitchen having tea. Nick could not make eye contact with Maddie no matter how much she stared at him. Figures, she thought.

"Maddie," Rosie began as she bit into a croissant. "I was wondering if you would consider joining us at our wedding. It's been so lovely to meet you and we would be thrilled to have you here with us," Rosie said with a smile. Oliver put his arm around Rosie and smiled at her, as if she was the most angelic creature he had ever seen.

Maddie squinted her eyes, looking between her and Nick. Nick could still not look at her. Pursing her lips, Maddie considered her options. She could politely decline and insist she had other sightseeing to do, which she really did not. Or, she mused, she could make Nick entirely uncomfortable.

Taking a sip of her tea, Maddie smiled and looked up at Rosie. "That would be incredible, Rosie. That's so sweet of you to invite me. You wouldn't want to go dress shopping with me, would you?"

Rosie squealed and stood up to hug Maddie. "I am so excited you are coming!" She said. "I know the perfect shop to take you to find one. With your figure, you'll have no problem finding a stunning dress."

Maddie smiled and hugged Rosie back. "I can't wait," she said sincerely.

Breakfast continued with friendly chatter. She heard the screeching of a woman shouting greetings from the front entry and nearly fell off of her stool when her friend from the plane ride over here, Gladys, walked into the room. Gladys, whose fiery red hair was perfectly coiffed, dropped her bags on the floor when she spotted Maddie.

"Well, if it isn't the model's girl! Whatever are you doing here?" She shouted with her strong accent as she waddled over to Maddie.

Maddie blushed as Gladys came over to hug her. "That didn't quite work out," she said. "What are you doing here?" She asked Gladys.

"This is Aunt Gladys," Rosie said, interrupting their reunion.

"No way!" Maddie said with a laugh. "I met Gladys on the plane over here."

"We became fast friends," Gladys said with a smile.

"She came here with Nick," Rosie said. Gladys and Rosie exchanged conspiratorial looks and nodded.

"Interesting," Gladys said. She moved on to greeting the rest of the family, kissing Nick on both cheeks and pulling on his beard. "Oh Nicky, when are you going to trim this beard? Tell me you will before the wedding. Your poor mother will keel over if you look this scruffy in all the photos." He blushed and pulled away from Gladys, a smile on his face.

"I'll think about it," he said gruffly.

After Gladys got settled in, Rosie invited her along with Maddie and Doreen to go dress shopping. Gladys excitedly agreed, liberally buttering a croissant before munching on it.

While Maddie sat quietly and sipped her tea, she found Nick staring at her intently, a frown on his face. She intentionally sat across from him, the seat next to him now taken up by Gladys. She gave him a curt smile and continued listening to the conversation.

Shortly after, the women piled into the Rolls Royce. Maddie and Doreen sat in the backseat with Rosie and Gladys up front. As soon as they left the property, Gladys reached out to turn off the radio and turned around swiftly. With a serious look on her face, she narrowed her eyes at Maddie and said, "Okay girly, tell me everything."

Maddie gulped and blushed. She decided to be honest with them, and told them everything—well, not *everything*—about Calum and how Nick was kind enough to let her stay in Rosie's flat. She explained how Nick invited her to come along for his trip, and how they got along well. The women all smiled and nodded knowingly, as if they could sense that there was something more than friendship.

"Well you know," Gladys began, "Nick hasn't brought home a woman in ages. Ever since that terrible—."

"Auntie," Rosie said swiftly, cutting her off. She shook her head and Gladys nodded, changing the subject. "What kind of dress do you think you'd like, Maddie?" she said, her voice changing and turning lighter.

Maddie was puzzled at what Gladys said. What was she about to say? What was terrible? Instead of prying, she began talking about different types of dresses, not really caring much about what she wore.

At the shop, Maddie tried on what seemed like dozens of dresses. When she slipped on a long sleeved, dark blue silky dress, Maddie knew it was the one. Small gemstones lined the décolletage. When she turned around in the figure-clinging, long dress, her entire back was exposed. She liked the way her body dipped and curved in the dress, hugging her just right.

The women *oohed* and *ahhed* when she modeled it for them, and she knew it was the one. After finding a pair of heels covered in similar gemstones, Maddie took everything up to the counter. She pulled out her credit card that she saved for emergencies, and was about to hand it to the cashier before Rosie cut in next to her, handing the clerk some cash.

"It's a gift, from Oliver and I," Rosie said with a smile.

"Oh, really, I couldn't—" Maddie began.

"Don't worry about it, Mads," Rosie said, using the nickname that Melissa had for her. "You can buy us lunch," she said with a smile.

Maddie was more than happy with that deal, and excitedly carried the beautiful dress outside to the car.

A few minutes later, they pulled into the parking lot of a pizza place. "Is this Oliver's restaurant?" Maddie asked as they stepped out of the car.

"Yes," Rosie said. "As a connoisseur of pizza, you"ll have to give him your honest opinion,"she said with a laugh as she held the door for the women.

After a delicious lunch, in which there was no charge given that it was Rosie and her family, Maddie was more confident than ever about agreeing to join in on the wedding. Although things with her and Nick were clearly in an odd place, she was still determined to have the best time.

The rest of the day went by fast. The women drove around town running some last-minute errands before the wedding. They had to pick up the wedding favors from a shop and finalize the details for the wedding cake.

On the way back to the house, Rosie peered in the rearview mirror to Maddie. "How would you like to come to my hen party with me tonight?" she asked. "It will be fun. All of my friends are teachers. We will have a grand time."

Maddie pondered it and decided it did indeed sound like fun. "I'd like that," she said. "Thank you so much for thinking of me."

"You girls better not get yourselves into any trouble," Doreen said in a motherly tone.

"I have no idea why she didn't invite us," Gladys said jokingly.

"It's because you'd be the one who brings the male strippers along, Auntie!" Rosie said, laughing hard. Gladys squealed and the entire car erupted in laughter.

Returning His Love

Chapter 14

Since it was going to be a late night, the girls decided to take afternoon naps before getting ready for dinner. Maddie carefully hung up her dress in the closet, then fell onto the bed.

Not able to sleep, she read a book on her phone and checked her work email. When a message from Shannon popped up, she quickly read it.

"Mel is so worried about you!" she said. "What's happening?"

She typed back a quick reply. "I am just having some fun," Maddie said. "Tell Melissa not to worry. I am having the best time ever!"

"I'll try to tell her," Shannon said, "But you know how protective she is. She is driving Jakob nuts with theories of who that giant bearded man is. I told her it's probably Jakob's long lost Scottish brother and she didn't think that was very funny."

Maddie laughed at that and then signed off for the afternoon, forcing herself to rest her eyes for a bit. She was looking forward to an old-fashioned girls night. Rosie assured her it would be super low-key with just dinner and some drinks.

An hour or so later, she got up and straightened her hair. It was a mess, but she did her best. Digging in her suitcase for an outfit that would be appropriate for a girls night out, she found the yellow sweater dress that she wore for her night out with Calum and slipped it on. If she wasn't mistaken, it was a little tight on her. She stretched it out a bit, not wanting to look like a complete hussy with the way it clung to her chest.

After reapplying the lipstick, Maddie walked downstairs to find the family in the sitting room. The women all complimented her outfit. Rosie looked adorable in a trim white pantsuit with a "bachelorette" sash.

Nick took a swig of the beer he was drinking, then stared deeply into Maddie's eyes. She wasn't sure whether he was angry or turned on, or perhaps a combination of the two.

The girls quickly departed, rushing off to a nearby pub where they met Rosie's friends. Five cosmos and a delicious dinner of fish and chips later, Maddie and Rosie stumbled out to the Uber, linking each other's arms and laughing. They had a lovely evening with her friends, and Maddie felt like it was the first time in a while that she really let loose.

When they arrived back at the estate, the two did their best to quietly make it up the stairs. Unfortunately, they were apparently both clumsy and were not the quietest. After a few fits of giggles, they said good night, Rosie slipping into her and Oliver's room down the hall.

Just as Maddie was about to enter her room, Nick's door flew open. "Maddie?" He asked into the darkness.

"Nicholas!" Maddie screeched, a little too loud.

"Thank fook, you're back safe," he said, clearly relieved. Nick walked out into the hallway, shirtless and just in his boxers.

"Of course I am back safe," Maddie retorted. "What did you think I was going to do?"

"I don't even want to think about it," he said.

"We should go inside if you want to talk," Maddie said. "We wouldn't want to wake anyone up."

"Good idea," Nick said, slipping into her room behind her and shutting the door.

Maddie turned on the gas fireplace and went into the bathroom to change. Slipping off the dress, she threw on a pair of leggings and a sweatshirt. She felt a bit wobbly with the alcohol. Walking out, Nick sat on her bed, his hard body covered in tattoos.

"You looked stunning tonight," he said sincerely.

"Thank you," Maddie replied curtly. She slipped under the covers and he turned around to face her, one foot off of the bed.

"What's wrong?" He asked her.

'What do you mean?" she said, staring at his tattoos. At this angle she could see the tattoos that curved around his upper arm. In the firelight, she could make out the deep imprint of a flag flying high in the wind with the year 1984 printed on it. She was curious about the date. Was it the year he was born? No, Maddie realized, doing the math in her head. Nick would have been born in 1982. Before she could think about it more, Maddie hiccuped and then looked over at Nick.

"You seem different today, off," he explained.

"I heard you and Rosie talking this morning, in the hall," she admitted.

Shaking his head, Nick sighed heavily. "I didn't mean for anybody to hear that, Maddie," he said. "You have to understand, my family—."

"Don't worry about it, Nick," she said. "We are just friends. I get it. It was my fault for thinking anything else."

"It's not that," Nick whispered, his voice strained. "You have to understand. I can't be anything more to you than a friend. That's all we can be."

Maddie didn't get it, but she was too sleepy from the alcohol to fight with him on the matter. "It's fine, Nick. We will be friends. It's all we ever were. Even if you're the hottest man I've ever seen in my entire life. Friends can fool around, right?" Maddie asked as she reached over to try to pull Nick closer.

Before she could reach him, Nick stood up and walked backwards away from the bed.

"Nicholas, come back," Maddie said dramatically. "Come touch me. I want to see you naked again."

"Not when you're drunk," he said seriously, reaching forward only to tuck the sheets over her body.

Minutes seemed to pass before Nick walked towards the door. "Goodnight, love," he whispered as he shut the door. "Sleep well."

The next morning, Maddie quickly realized that as much of a fan as she was of Scottish tea, it was not going to cut it for the hangover she was nursing. She did not get up until ten o'clock. When she made it downstairs, she found Rosie on the couch with a pillow over her head. After making a pot of coffee, she settled in next to Rosie and the two laughed about the night before.

She discovered that Nick and Oliver were outside by the barn. He was helping Oliver repair some of the fencing. Gladys and Doreen were out getting the final alterations done on their dresses.

Thinking about Nick brought memories flooding back to last night, when Maddie practically begged Nick to touch her. How mortifying!

Maddie decided that she had had enough social interaction for a few days. Rosie encouraged her to spend the day in bed. The only plans Rosie had for the day were to go to the salon later for a manicure. Maddie wasn't big on salons so she turned down her invitation. Finding some crackers in the enormous pantry, Maddie walked upstairs and tucked herself into bed.

She enjoyed spending the afternoon immersed in books that she had been meaning to read for ages. The bedroom made her feel like a royal who could spend her days reading if she so chose. Smiling, she opened up another book on her phone as she munched on crackers.

Maddie was certain that there was nothing she enjoyed more than reading in bed. That is, until she found a remote on the side table. Picking it up, Maddie looked around. She did not see a television anywhere in sight. Looking at the remote, she pressed an arrow button. There, from the end of the bed, a television set emerged from the wood. Maddie's jaw dropped as she watched the TV rise up. Was this some sort of dream?

Turning the television on, she quickly found reruns of the the UK's version of *The Bachelor,* which immediately seemed so much juicier than the one back home, if only because of all the accents.

Maddie sat enthralled for hours, only leaving the bed to get more water and go to the bathroom. She found herself still in her pajamas at four in the afternoon.

Around five, a knock on the door startled her out of her obsession with discovering who would get the final rose. "Come in," she called out.

Nick walked in, a tray in front of him. Maddie began to blush at the sight of him, embarrassed at how she acted.

"Rosie said you weren't feeling too well," he began. "I made you some soup."

"Weren't you outside building fences all day?" Maddie asked curiously.

"Yes," Nick said. "Then I came in and made this. It's chicken noodle. I hope you like it."

"It smells amazing," she said. "Thank you." Maddie was constantly take aback by how considerate he was. "About last night..." Maddie began.

"Don't worry about it, love," Nick said genuinely. "I'm glad you had a good time with my sister."

"She is lovely," Maddie said. "I'm embarrassed at my behavior. I should have controlled myself."

"I get it," Nick said. "You just can't keep your hands off me," he said jokingly.

"Something like that," she muttered, then turned her attention to the tray.

As she sipped on the soup which was, like everything Nick cooked, delicious, they sat in silence as they watched the finale of the show. It included lots of kissing, crying, and an engagement ring. Maddie's broken heart did flip flops inside her.

After the show ended, Maddie turned off the TV and sent it back down into the bed.

"Are you getting excited for the wedding?" She asked.

"Yes," Nick said. "It will be nice to see family. We are going to all go over there tomorrow. All the guests are staying over at the castle," Nick said.

Maddie's blue eyes grew wide as she thought about staying in one of the rooms. "Even me?" she asked.

"Yes, of course," Nick said.

"It sounds lovely," she admitted. She could not resist her excitement for the event. She had never been around such lush extravagance before, and was more than happy to take it all in.

Maddie continued to sip on her soup. Nick watched her with attentive eyes, lips pulled together as if he wanted to tell her something but did not know how to go about it.

Instead, Nick told her that he better go see to everyone else and catch up with Gladys. Maddie thanked him again for the soup. She decided that a hot bath was what she needed before going to bed early.

As she soaked in the tub, she could not help but think of their night together at the cabin. Everything seemed so right that night, as if they were meant to be together. Although she was disappointed with Nick for his behavior and insistence that they remain just friends, Maddie could not deny her attraction to him. There was just something about him that made her wanting to keep coming back for more. She didn't know whether it was his protective nature, or that he did such kind things for her, or maybe just the fact that he really was one of the most attractive men she had ever seen.

Regardless, he managed to be the first thing on her mind in the mornings and the last thing she thought about before falling asleep, and Maddie did not want that to end anytime soon.

Chapter 15

The day before the wedding went by in a daze. Everyone was hustling to the get to the castle and to greet the guests. Maddie spent the morning hanging garland with Gladys as Oliver and Rosie greeted family members and showed them to their rooms.

She and Gladys worked well together, each having the same perfectionist eye for detail. Nick remained busy bringing everyone's luggage in and making sure people were settled. With over 350 guests expected, they were in for a big weekend. The small cottages on the property were also going to be filled with family and friends.

Maddie kept herself busy throughout the day and only realized that it was dinner time when her stomach growled. Rosie came in to get Maddie and show her the room she would be staying in. As they climbed the magnificent staircase, Maddie spent time looking at all the antiquities and enormous paintings. This castle was everything she ever dreamed of and more.

As they walked down the large hallway, family bustled in and out of everyone's rooms, smiling and laughing. Rosie directed her to the last room at the end of the hall.

Inside, she found a small, quaint room with gorgeous features. The red walls were meticulously decorated with portraits of years past. A stunning gold chandelier hung from the ceiling. A modest bed was perched on one wall. Maddie walked into the bathroom and found a clawfoot tub in the center of the room. The old tub was offset by a modern shower and vanity. Once again, Maddie was in heaven.

"I can't thank you enough for inviting me," Maddie said to a beaming Rosie.

"It's our pleasure," Rosie said as she walked towards the door. "Any friend of Nick is a friend of ours." After relaying dinner plans for the night, Rosie left Maddie to get ready. She wondered what Nick was doing, and wished she could see him.

After changing into a red skirt and an oversized cable-knit sweater, Maddie headed downstairs to meet everyone for the bus to the restaurant for dinner. Two large buses were parked outside. Maddie made friendly conversation with the guests, happy to meet some of Nick's relatives. She made her way on the bus, looking for any sign of Nick.

Not seeing him, she took a seat and listened to the chatter going on around her. Suddenly, Maddie had the urge to look up. Standing at the head of the bus was Nick, eyes frantically scanning the bus. When he caught her gaze, he let out a breath and came down the aisle to sit next to her.

Maddie was overwhelmed by the feeling of being in his presence. He looked dapper in black slacks and a dark blue v-neck sweater. She did not think she had ever seen him so dressed up. If she wasn't mistaken, she could have sworn that his beard was a bit shorted, the frizzled ends cleaned up a bit. She smiled as she looked over at him.

"Hi Nicholas," she said. "How was your day?"

"It was good," Nick said, nervously turning towards her. "What about you?"

"It was so fun," Maddie said honestly. "I really enjoy spending time with Gladys. We are kindred spirits. I want to be just like her when I'm her age."

"Please, no," Nick said with a laugh. The two chuckled about Gladys and discussed her daughter in Chicago, who Gladys had just been visiting. Nick said that he had never been to the States before, but his Mum was hoping to get a chance to go visit his cousin soon and he promised that he would tag along.

She tried to calm her heart down as she thought about the possibility of Nick being so close to her home that they could meet up. As just friends, of course.

"You're invited to Willow Falls anytime," Maddie said sweetly. "I'd love to show you around. You could meet my sister and see my library."

Nick looked down at Maddie and grinned. "That sounds great, Maddie. It would be an honor."

She smiled through the entire ride to the restaurant. They all piled out of the bus and into one of Oliver's more upscale restaurants. The entire place was reserved just for the wedding guests. Nick pulled

Maddie over to the head table, where he sat next to Rosie. He insisted she sit next to him. Blushing, Maddie took a seat. Down the table, she recognized Nick's redhead cousin-in-law from the coffee shop and they exchanged smiles and a wave. The woman appeared surprised that Nick had a date.

They enjoyed a delicious meal of shrimp and lobster. Maddie was certain that she may have an addiction to drawn butter. At one point, Nick reached out to swipe a bit of butter from the corner of her mouth. Before he could stop himself, he dipped his finger between his lips, sucking off the butter.

"Delicious," he said to her under his breath. Maddie blushed as he pulled his finger out of his mouth and went back to eating as if nothing at all had happened. She looked up to find Gladys sitting across from the table, starting at them with her mouth open. Maddie blushed even harder when Gladys picked up the fork she had dropped and then proceeded to wink at Maddie.

By the time dinner was over, everyone seemed pretty tired. On the ride back, Nick talked to her about the cottage he was staying in. Maddie described her room and how perfect it was. When they got off the bus, Nick pointed to where his cottage was located down a trail to the side of the lake and Maddie nodded.

They said their goodbyes and went their separate ways for the night. Maddie was thrilled for the wedding. She was not sure if she was more excited to see the ceremony or to see Nick in a tuxedo. With that thought, she fell fast asleep and did not stir again until her alarm woke her up the next morning.

Breakfast was delivered to everyone's rooms so that people could get ready leisurely without feeling the need to get all dressed up in the morning. Maddie took her dress out of its bag and set it up on a hanger in the bathroom. She took a long, leisurely steam shower and spent extra time lathering her skin and shaving her legs. The steam from the shower released any wrinkles in her dress. She felt luxurious in the state-of-the-art shower and would have died to have one of her own.

Tugging on a puffy white robe, Maddie sat down on the chaise lounge and relaxed while she sipped her coffee. Around midmorning, Maddie began doing her hair and makeup. She settled on a simple updo for her hair, her blonde locks swept up in a braided bun.

Maddie carefully applied her makeup, opting for a sparkly eyeshadow to top everything off. As she slipped on her dress, she felt more elegant than ever before. The dress was absolutely perfect and fit her like a glove.

She tiptoed over to the room across the hall. Gladys opened the door, her hair in curlers. "Well, lovie, you look gorgeous!" Gladys said, glowing when she saw Maddie's dress.

"Thanks, Gladys," Maddie said. "I was hoping you could zip me up?" She asked.

"Only if you return the favor, dearie," Gladys said. She hustled Maddie into the room and carefully zipped up her dress. Tearing off her robe, Gladys unveiled a bright pink dress with dozens of tulle layers. It clashed incredibly with her red hair, and yet Maddie could not think of another person who could pull it off.

"You look amazing!" Maddie said sincerely. Gladys smiled as she turned around. Maddie had a hell of time getting the dress zipped, but when the task was finally completed, Gladys let out a breath and looked at herself in the mirror.

"I feel as young as you!" she said, smiling as she began to take her curlers off.

"You look it, too," Maddie said, collecting the curlers for Gladys as she took them out.

"I'm so happy for Rosie," Gladys said. "She is so happy with Oliver. He's such a nice young man. I was so worried that Rosie would never find someone. She's practically middle aged now!"

Maddie laughed. "Isn't she only thirty-five?"

"Yes, poor girl," Gladys said *tsk*ing. "Don't even get me started on Nicholas. Nearly thirty-eight and still not settled down. I worry about him," she admitted.

Maddie nodded. "I understand. They are really lucky to have you, Gladys. I would have given anything to have an aunt like you growing up."

"You didn't have aunts?" Gladys asked.

"No," Maddie said. "My family was very dysfunctional growing up. It's a long story, and a sad one, but my father is the reason that my mother is dead," she explained solemnly.

"Oh my dear!" Gladys exclaimed. "You poor thing. What a terrible thing for a young girl like you to go through. It's no wonder that Nick has taken you under his wing. You are such a beautiful young girl, and so confident. I could tell right when I met you that you are going places. A person would never guess what you've been through."

"I guess the therapy worked then," Maddie joked.

A knock on the door interrupted their conversation. Gladys' husband opened the door and raised his eyebrows at his wife.

"You look positively ravishing, darling," he said, strolling in to clutch her wide hips lovingly.

"Well thank you, dear," Gladys said. Looking at Maddie, she asked them both, "Well, should we go downstairs?"

As they made their way down the staircase, Maddie watched the crowds of well-dressed people make their way into the grand ballroom.

Maddie followed Gladys and her husband into the ballroom. Everything looked positively magical. Hundreds of seats were set up facing the altar. Lights twinkled all around them. The pink and white flowers looked gorgeous and covered the entire room. The strong scent of flowers wafted into Maddie's nostrils as she took a seat on one of the chairs. Gladys and her husband settled in next to her.

After ten or so minutes of chatter, the room quieted down and everyone was seated. The bagpipes began to sound as Oliver's parents came down the aisle, then the bridesmaids, who looked beautiful in pink.

Following them came the groomsmen. Maddie did a double-take when they walked in with kilts on. She cursed herself for being so silly as to forget that men wore kilts at Scottish weddings and not tuxedoes. Oliver looked dashing as he came down the aisle, no sign of nerves at all.

Fantasies of Nick in a kilt were soon realized when he walked in the room and began to stride down the aisle. He looked absolutely ravishing in the black fitted jacket and gray tartan kilt. Tall boots with black socks came up to his knees. Maddie could see bits of his leg tattoos poking out above the socks and smiled. She loved knowing what was beneath his clothes.

Nick looked stoic as he walked down the aisle, only smiling when he made his way to the altar and saw his parents. His parents came to the front and Doreen spent a moment getting Nick's father situated in the wheelchair. Doreen sat down next to a chair that was empty except for a single white rose. Maddie assumed that it must be for one of Nick's grandparents.

The crowd gasped and everyone stood when Rosie came into the room and began to walk slowly down the aisle. She looked absolutely stunning in a traditional long-sleeved wedding gown, the delicate lace accentuating her curves in all the right places. The train was very long, and two young girls diligently carried it down the aisle. Doreen stood up to help Rosie adjust her train once she got to the altar. Once everyone was situated, Maddie noticed Oliver wiping a tear away from his cheek.

Once the ceremony began, Maddie found herself stealing glances at Nick. He looked immensely proud to be standing up next to his sister. With his hands behind his back, his large chest protruded out of the fitted jacket. Maddie's heart beat faster the longer she looked at him in the kilt, and insisted on paying attention to the ceremony instead of looking at him. She couldn't handle the distraction.

Once the vows were said and the happy couple sealed them with a kiss, Maddie was unsure if there was a dry eye in the room. The two were so clearly in love that it made Maddie so happy to watch them commit to each other. When Oliver slid the ring on Rosie's finger, she nearly swooned over how romantic it was.

After the kiss, everyone in the room cheered and clapped. Maddie was certain that by the time the joyous moment was over, she'd hugged nearly all the guests. Everyone made their way to the open area of the castle to enjoy drinks and hors d'oeuvres while workers turned the ballroom into a dining area and dance floor.

Maddie had just gotten a glass of wine from the bar when she swirled around to find Nick behind her. It was one thing to see him in the kilt from afar, and another thing altogether to be this close to a highlander in the flesh.

"Good gravy," she muttered as she shamelessly looked at him up and down.

"Maddie," Nick said quietly, just loud enough for her to hear over the orchestra and chatter in the room. "You look so fooking perfect right now," he said. "You've never been more beautiful."

Maddie blushed furiously at the compliment, then said to him. "I could say the same thing about you."

Nick stood up to his full height, and stared down at her, looking at her as if he was not sure if she was poking fun at him.

"I'm serious," she said. "You look really handsome in that. I could hardly pay attention to the ceremony."

"The feeling is mutual," he said, his blue eyes roaming up and down her body.

"You're taller," he said. Maddie was tall to begin with, but with the heels she stood over six feet. With the typical man, she would be towering over them. In this case, she didn't even reach Nick's eyes.

Maddie pointed down to her heels and nodded. Nick grabbed a whiskey from the bar, then led Maddie by the elbow to a corner. "I meant what I said," Nick said. "You really do look amazing."

"Thanks, *friend*," Maddie said, resisting the urge to playfully punch him in the arm.

Nick scowled at her words, then took a swig of the drink.

"You can't just pick and choose when you want to flirt with me and when you want to be my friend," Maddie continued, feeling more confident with every sip of her wine. "That's really shitty behavior, you know," she asserted.

"We may have started out as friends, love, but you and I both know that we've felt a lot more than just friendly with each other."

"So what's the problem?" Maddie asked, getting frustrated with his behavior. One moment, they were just friends. The next, he wanted to be with her.

"The problem is," Nick said, switching to a glass of water "I can't be with anyone, even if it is what I want more than anything in the world."

"Why the hell not?" Maddie asked, picking up a glass of water that Nick handed her. "Why can't you be with me or anybody else?" She set the glass down on a table and crossed her arms, her cleavage spilling over her arms.

Nick drank the rest of the water and then set the glass down as well with more force than necessary. "I don't want to talk about that," he said. "I just want you to know that it has nothing to do with you."

"Oh, it has nothing to do with me?" Maddie scoffed. "Why would it anyway? I'm just a young girl from America. Listen, you," she said, pointing her finger at him. "If you think that I'm going to be your pity friend, you're sorely mistaken. If you think you can feel all macho and knight in shining armor by showing me around Scotland, well fine. But I can get back on a plane at any time and leave all this behind!" Maddie said, her finger shaking as she pointed it at him.

Nick gently reached out and pulled her hand down, squeezing it in his big hand. "I never meant to hurt you," Nick said. "I'm sorry." He looked genuinely hurt, as if the thought of losing her hit him for the first time.

"No, I'm sorry," Maddie said. "I'm sorry for catching feelings for you."

Before he could reply, Rosie came running up to them. "Come on you two!" She said cheerfully. "We are having a quick dance before dinner.

Nick nearly groaned but followed his sister dutifully, still clutching Maddie's hand. When they entered the ballroom, it had been transformed into a dining area with dozens of tables. The dance floor was in the center, with Rosie rushing in to dance with Oliver. Doreen was sitting on Elliot's lap as he spun them around in a circle. They were both laughing uncontrollably as the upbeat music played on. Other couples began filing into the dance floor.

Nick sighed heavily and dragged Maddie along with him onto the dance floor. Maddie smiled as Nick tried but failed miserably to dance along to the upbeat music. For a moment, she was able to forget his shameful behavior in order to laugh at him.

Just as Nick was starting to get into the rhythm, the song ended and a slow song began. Nick wasted no time wrapping Maddie in his arms and bringing her close to him. As frustrated as she was, she couldn't help but slide right into his arms, feeling his warmth. She could smell the whiskey on his breath mixed with his woodsy, utterly male scent.

As they danced together, slowly moving to the music, Maddie felt as if she was home, and she hated herself for that feeling. She knew it would be fleeting, and that nothing could ever possibly come of this pairing. And yet, she wanted nothing more than to be with Nick, even if only for one more night.

As the song came to an end, Maddie realized that her breathing was shaky as she moved to step away from Nick. Clearing her throat, she strode towards one of the front tables and took a seat.

Nick came and sat next to her, biting into a piece of bread and chewing it roughly. Nick poured them each a glass of water. As the food came around, members of the bridal party began giving speeches. Servers brought plates of food out and Maddie dug into the meal.

Rosie's girlfriends told funny stories of how infatuated she was with Oliver when she first met him and Oliver's friends told similar ones. Maddie nudged Nick during one of the speeches and asked him if he was going to say anything. Nick shook his head.

When it came around to Aunt Gladys' turn, she had everyone in stitches with her funny stories. Before she finished, she turned somber. "We all know that one very special person is missing today. I know that he would be the happiest fella here, so proud of Rosie and all that she's become. I 'ave no doubt that he's looking down on us from Heaven and smiling." There was not a dry eye in the room by the time that Gladys was done talking.

Maddie looked around, clearly confused. She had no idea who Gladys was talking about, and was not about to ask Nick, who was pressing his fingers against his eyes as if to try to stop them from tearing up.

After finishing the meal, the happy couple cut the cake and it was served. Maddie ate the cake quietly as she listened to the chatter around the table. She looked at the cake on Nick's plate, still untouched. He held his water glass tightly, staring out at the dance floor where Oliver and Rosie were dancing once again.

Maddie went to chat with some of Rosie's friends but couldn't help but keep looking back at Nick. She didn't know what was going on. When she made it back to the table, Nick was in the same position, the tight jacket straining as he leaned forward on the table, his mind somewhere far away.

Leaning in, Maddie swiped a bit of the buttercream frosting from Nick's piece of cake and put it in her mouth, licking it off of her finger. Nick looked up at her, breaking his stare for the first time in minutes.

Unexpectedly, he smiled at her. Then swiping a bit of the frosting himself, he held his finger up to her lips, rubbing it on Maddie's bottom lip. Maddie bit down on her bottom lip, swiping her tongue to lick it up.

Nick stifled a groan as he watched her. He was done for. "Let's get out of here," he said quietly. Maddie nodded, then drank as much of her water as she could.

Returning His Love

Chapter 16

They escaped out of the ballroom without anyone noticing. Nick took his jacket off and put it around Maddie's shoulders, then opened the front doors and they walked down the path to the cottage he was staying in.

He clutched her hand tightly and she eagerly kept up with Nick's tall stride. When they made it to the cottage, he unzipped the pouch on the front of his kilt and pulled out the key. Nick opened the door and let Maddie go in first. The cottage was quaint, with a big bed and more than enough room for the two of them.

Maddie slid off the jacket and hung it up as Nick went to start a fire. She was cozy and entirely comfortable but definitely nervous. When she was alone with Nick, it was like no place else in the world existed.

Nick turned to Maddie, then led her over to a couch. When they took a seat next to each other, Maddie moved closer to him. She wanted to be closer to him, no matter what that meant.

"Maddie," Nick said. "Words cannot describe how much I want to be with you. But I can't promise you forever, or happily ever after, or anything else that you deserve. The only thing I can promise you is tonight."

Maddie nodded. As much as she did not understand what was really going on, she knew that there was something so incredibly broken inside Nick that prevented him from being able to handle anything more. Would she like to be with Nick? Of course. Since that was not a possibility, Maddie was going to jump at the next best thing: one night with him.

"I know," Maddie said. "I'm okay with it."

"You are?" Nick asked incredulously.

She nodded. "Yes. I want you to have everything. Please unzip me," she said, standing up and turning around so that her back was facing him.

Nick let out a breath, then stood up behind her. Maddie could feel the warmth of his body on her exposed back. She longed to feel his skin on her skin. He unzipped the zipper that trailed down her lower back down her bottom. His hands grazed her ass as she slid the dress off her arms and it fell to the floor. Maddie kicked her heels off and stepped out of the dress, her lacy black bra and panty set contrasting against the paleness of her skin.

Nick tore the shirt off of his body, letting the kilt drop to the floor. He quickly pulled off the boots and socks. Soon, he was standing in front of Maddie in only his underwear. His thick cock protruded behind the tight black underwear so tantalizingly that Maddie wanted to reach out and cup it.

Maddie pushed a stray hair out of her face, tucking it behind her ear. She was nervous. Although they had just been in the same position just a few days before, somehow this felt so much more real.

She walked up to Nick, placing her hands on his chest. She traced the details of his tattoos over and over again, getting lost in the maze of ink.

Nick leaned down and placed his hand underneath Maddie's chin. Tipping it up, he leaned down and kissed her deeply. Maddie leaned into the kiss, never wanting it to end.

Nick reached down to lift Maddie up, gently placing her on the bed. Before he could lay down next to her, she urged him to take his boxers off. Maddie slid her panties off. When she reached back to remove her bra, Nick pushed her hands away, distracting her with nips on her neck. Finding the clasp, he slipped the bra off of her. There they were, together, naked on the bed.

Maddie's heart beat fast as Nick leaned down and continued to kiss her, gently at first, then more fiercely. She climbed on top of his hips like once before, feeling his enormous cock between her legs.

Maddie's legs spread as she straddled him, feeling the pulse of his cock in her core. Nick reached up to gently cup her breasts. After a few more tender kisses, Nick flipped Maddie onto her back. As he perched above her, she smiled as he went to nip at her lower lip. He kissed a trail down to her neck, then in-between her breasts. His fingers massaged her nipples, gently pulling at the sensitive beads.

Maddie could hardly restrain her moans. The sensation was like nothing she was used to. He continued on, tugging and pulling between kisses. She let out a sigh when he stopped and move further downward. Grabbing her hips, he placed kisses around her stomach. The further down he got, the heavier Maddie began to breathe. She knew what was coming and she wanted it immensely.

Nick took his time before putting his mouth on her. He spent what seemed like ages kissing her legs, her hips, her thighs. He even licked the scar on her thigh from when she fell out of the tree. Maddie was exasperated with need. Her breath caught as she felt his hot mouth inching closer towards her.

When his lips finally met her most private place, she chanted his name loudly. His tongue worked wonders on her clit. Maddie tried to hold back from thrusting her pussy into his face. He grabbed her ass with both hands, lifting her up to get a better angle. Nick's tongue darted in and out of her pussy.

Maddie was already aroused before she got in bed with Nick. To have him touching her in such an intimate place was nearly too much to bear. "Wait," Maddie said as she felt herself getting close. Nick stilling, stopping all movement when she told him to hold off.

"I want to come with you inside me," Maddie said, a little shy about voicing what she wanted.

"Love, you will," he said. "I guarantee it. But I plan on making you come many times tonight, not just when I'm inside you." He brought his thumb down on top of her clit, then swirled it around dangerously slowly. Maddie lifted her hips off of the bed at this movement, wanting more and more.

The faster he moved his thumb, the more Nick moved his tongue inside of her. Burying his face deeper between her thighs, Nick gave her everything he had. Relentlessly, Maddie came once, then twice.

"Nick!" she screamed as the second wave of pleasure came over her.

Nick slowly withdrew his head and fingers, then scooted up the bed to be closer to Maddie. She was breathless, a glistening sheen of sweat on her brow.

"That was incredible," she said to him, clutching his bicep.

"Anything for you," Nick said. Maddie reached down for his cock, but Nick pulled away.

"No, no, no," he said. "Tonight is all about you."

Maddie smiled, then whimpered a bit. "But I love your cock," she whined.

"You'll love it more when it's deep inside you, I guarantee it," Nick said. Eyes widening at the thought, Maddie knew this moment was coming, but the idea of Nick's massive cock fitting inside of her was a tad bit nerve-wracking.

As his fingers began massaging her vulva, Nick worked his way towards her pussy. Slowly, he slipped one finger inside of her, gently moving it in and out of her. Maddie groaned at the sensation, her moans getting closer and closer together. He teased another finger near her entrance. Looking at Maddie, he waited for her nod before sliding the next finger inside of her.

"God, I love that," she admitted, biting her bottom lip.

"You like it when I fuck you with my fingers, little one?" Nick asked, leaning down to kiss her.

She nodded fervently. Maddie's pussy was dangerously wet, inching closer and closer to another orgasm. The feel of his thick fingers sliding in and out of her was enough to send her over the edge. When he brought his fingers closer together and pulled them in a "come hither" motion, Maddie had to hold back a scream. He was, indeed, giving her a g-spot orgasm, Maddie's first.

After she fought her way through the orgasm, trying to keep her screams to a minimum, Nick clutched her hand. "Are you ready for this?" he asked.

"Yes," she answered breathlessly.

Nick got off the bed and grabbed a condom from the bedside table. He tore open the package, then slid it on his cock in such a way that it looked like he was stroking himself.

Maddie nearly fainted at the sight of it and could not stop staring at his beautiful cock. Tan and long, thick veins ran along his cock, pulsing with blood and engorging the massive head even further. Nick crawled over on top of her and she leaned back, her head on the pillow. He ran his hands seductively down her body, then positioned his cock in front of her pussy. Maddie was never more ready for anything in her entire life. She felt surprisingly calm, and she knew that she was making the right decision.

Nick rubbed his cock up and down her pussy, letting her natural lubrication slick his cock. Slowly, he began to enter her. Maddie breathed heavily as she held onto Nick's biceps. He was so gentle with her. The sense of fullness and pressure as he pushed into her was a lot, and slightly painful, but more than anything, she felt immense pleasure.

Once he filled her to the hilt, he began to thrust in and out of her. Maddie moaned, her feminine gasps filling the room. Guttural noises emanated from Nick's throat as he began thrusting in her deeper, his cock harder than ever.

"Yes!" She screamed, loving feeling his cock work its way inside her, then pulling out, leaving her needing more. This was everything she ever thought it would be like and more. She craved for him to be closer to her, deeper inside of her.

Maddie felt the pressure build up inside her with another impending orgasm. Nick reached down between them and rubbed her clit as he continued to thrust. Suddenly, an orgasm overcame her. While she recovered, Nick leaned into her, catching her lips with his. As they furthered the kiss, Maddie reached out to rub the muscles of his chest.

Before long, Maddie felt another orgasm sweeping through her. As she began to come, Nick's breath grew shorter and shorter. Soon, he thrust in her five times with great force, moaning her name as he came. When they were able to catch their breaths from the orgasm, Nick leaned down to kiss her one last time. She was entirely sated.

He left the bed to dispose of his condom and get them each a glass of water. When he laid back down, Maddie curled up in front of him. He tucked his arm around her, pulling her close. As they fell asleep, Maddie's natural high prevented her from catching herself before she whispered, "I love you, Nicholas"

It was only when she heard the gruff, gravelly voice behind her say, "I love you, too" that she fell asleep, happier than she had ever been.

Maddie expected to wake up in Nick's arms, so when she woke up in the empty bed and—as she soon determined—an empty cottage. His suitcase was gone, too. She shook the sleep from her eyes, refusing to cry as she slipped her dress from last night back on. It was impossibly wrinkled and she had nobody to zip it up.

She told herself not to cry, that Nick was just somewhere in the castle. Maybe he was making her breakfast. Looking at the clock, it was nine in the morning. She assumed other guests would be up by now. Peeking out the window, the day was gray and windy. She could see the waves foaming up on Loch Ness.

Slipping her shoes on, Maddie walked down the path and to the castle, the wind hitting her face with deft ferocity. As she tiptoed in the front door, clutching the back of her dress closed. Maddie was halfway up the stairs to her room before looking downstairs. In the main dining room, she saw Nick's entire family looking up at her, concern in their eyes.

Maddie stormed up the stairs to her room, trying not to slam the door with any bit of the anger that she felt inside of her. Stripping the dress off, she ran towards the bathroom and turned the shower on as hot as it would go. She stepped into the shower, sliding down the wall and putting her head against her knees. The hot water pelted down on her back as Maddie cried, terribly concerned that she had just ruined everything.

Maddie eventually crawled out of the shower after washing her hair. She made an attempt of putting on makeup and brushing her hair. After throwing her clothes in the suitcase, Maddie tossed on a sweatshirt and some leggings.

Maddie turned on her phone, looking at her flight information back home. She was checking to see if there were any flights back to Chicago sooner. When she found one that was leaving at nine that night, she quickly switched out her ticket.

A knock at the door startled her as she was slipping her phone in her pocket. "Come in," she said, her voice rough and raw from crying. Doreen poked her head in and looked sadly at Maddie.

"Oh honey," she said, in the most motherly way. "What happened?" Before she could stop herself, Maddie put her head in her hands and started to cry. Doreen came over and sat next to Maddie on the bed, holding her as she cried.

A few minutes later, after catching her breath, Maddie asked Doreen if Nick was downstairs.

Doreen shook her head. "He took off early this morning," the kind woman explained. "He texted me and told me after I woke up."

"Where did he go?" Maddie asked, not understanding where Nick could possibly have to be at this hour the day after his sister's wedding.

"Back home, I'm sure," Doreen explained. "The only place Nick can really think through everything is in his wood shop."

"So he was just going to leave me here?" Maddie asked incredulously.

Doreen shook her head. "He asked me to have Gladys and Rick to take you back to the flat. He didn't say why," she continued. "They would be happy to drive you, of course. You're practically one of us now."

Maddie scoffed at that. "I thought I was, too," she said.

Doreen *tsk*ed and brushed the hair out of Maddie's face. "Nick has a lot of things that he still hasn't come to terms with. I am so sorry he hurt you," she said. "If I had my way, I'd give him a stern talking to for whatever he did, and I probably still will, but a thirty-seven year old only has to listen to his mother so much."

"I just don't understand why this has to be so hard," Maddie said, sniffling into a tissue.

"I suppose he didn't tell you about his brother?" Doreen asked quietly.

From the confused look on Maddie's face, Doreen took that as a sign to start from the beginning. "Nick had a little brother, Elliot Junior. He was two years younger than Nick, Rosie's twin. The boys did everything together, always getting into trouble. They were good boys, of course, and the spitting image of each other, but you know how boys are."

Maddie's brow furrowed as she listened to the story, shocked that any of this was true. How could she tell Nick everything about her life when he held out on her?

"Elliot was infatuated with the pub. He always wanted to take it over, coming up with ideas to get new people in. When they were teenagers, the boys worked in the pub. Elliot would put on ridiculous theme nights, having mini-golf tournaments, karaoke in the pub, you name it. The pub was never more popular. It was never really Nick's thing. He always wanted to focus on woodworking. That was his passion.

One night, when Nick was twenty and Elliot was eighteen, the boys went out with their friends. They hung around some shady friends, but I knew that Nick would always take care of Elliot. He's always been protective. Well, the two got on a motorbike and started racing. Nick was driving it, with Elliot sitting behind them. The roads were slick, and Nick hit a curve too fast. Our Elliot didn't make it," Doreen said, dabbing the corner of her eye with the sleeve of her sweater.

"Oh no!" Maddie said, feeling terrible for his family. That's when Nick's tattoo came flashing back to her. 1984—two years after Nick was born. The tattoo was for Elliot.

"Nick has never been the same. None of us blame him. It was an accident, of course, but Nick isn't the type to give up responsibility. The spark in his eye is gone. He's been punishing himself for Elliot's death for seventeen years. I don't know how he does it. I want to shake him sometimes," Doreen began, her voice faltering. "I want to tell him that he's still here, and that he needs to live. For Elliot. But he won't."

"I don't know what to say," Maddie said. She felt terrible that Nick was carrying around the weight of something that was clearly an accident.

"The only time I saw that spark come back in his eyes was when he was with you. Ask Gladys. Ask Rosie. Ask anyone. We haven't seen that Nick in ages. It was so good to have him back. I'm sorry he hurt you, Maddie," Doreen said. "I hope you'll give him some time. Maybe he will come around," Doreen said.

The women stood up and hugged each other. "I wish I had more time," Maddie said, shrugging. This was too much for her to take in right now, and she needed time to digest everything that had happened.

Doreen walked quietly out of the room, nodding as she left. Maddie was grateful for Doreen telling her the truth, but it unfortunately only complicated things.

Maddie knew that she agreed with him that they would only be together for one night only. She knew that she should not have told him that she loved him, but he said it back! What man left a woman after professing his love to her and taking her virginity? She shook her head, and carried her suitcase down the castle steps.

She ignored the sympathetic glances from Nick's extended family members, and instead took the hug that Rosie offered. She thanked them over and over for inviting her and insisted that she had a good time.

Walking over to Gladys, who pulled away from Doreen, she plastered a fake smile on her face, grabbed Maddie by the shoulder, and said, "Well I understand you are our travel partner!" Gladys hiked Maddie's suitcase in her arms, ignoring that it was a wheeling bag, and carried it outside.

After saying her reluctant goodbyes to the rest of Nick's family, she got in the backseat of Gladys and Rick's SUV. The drive was mostly silence, and she stared out the window at the foggy highlands.

When they made their way back to Glasgow, Maddie asked Gladys to drop her off at the airport. While she looked confused, Gladys did as she asked. When they arrived at the departures gate, Maddie gave Gladys and Rick a sad hug.

Making her way in the airport, Maddie checked her bag and got one last cup of tea. She had a few hours before her flight was going to leave, and she spent it with her eyes closed, trying to think about anything but Nick.

When Maddie was finally in the air, she sent an email to her sister. The title was "Surprise!" She wrote, "Hey Sis, Surprise! I'm coming home a week early. I will see you back in Willow Falls in just a matter of hours, really. I can't wait to see you. I miss you all. XOXO."

She pressed "send" then turned off her phone. Sleeping the rest of the journey, Maddie could not wait to get back home.

Returning His Love

Chapter 17

When the shuttle finally dropped Maddie off at her apartment complex, she was so exhausted that she wasn't sure whether she could walk the pathway to her door. Wisconsin was much colder than Scotland, and she trudged through three inches of snow to get inside.

As she walked up to her door, she heard the blare of her television from inside the apartment. When she entered the apartment, she found Hazel sitting on her couch in a long sleeve muumuu, a floral headscarf wrapped around her gray hair.

Hazel glanced at Maddie and turned the TV off right as the talk show host erupted into a scathing review of the current political system.

"Hey girl! You're home early. What's wrong? You look terrible!" Hazel said as she tucked a pack of cigarettes into the pocket of her muumuu, her raspy voice speaking only the truth.

"I feel it too," Maddie said, kicking the door shut and lugging her bag in. "I need a shower and about twelve hours of sleep," she told her neighbor.

"Okay, hon, do you want me to put some tea on for you?"

"No!" Maddie shouted as she walked into the bathroom, stripping off her clothes. When she emerged from her shower, Hazel was gone. When her doorbell rang, she ran over to the door. Inside was her deliveryman from her favorite pizza place.

"You're back!" he said to her. "We missed you."

"I missed you guys, too" Maddie said. "But I didn't order pizza."

"The old lady upstairs did," the college kid explained. "She said you looked like you really needed it."

Maddie let out a laugh and grabbed the box, handing the kid a tip from the jar she kept by the door.

Maddie carried the box to her bedroom, crawling in her bed and letting out a sigh at the comfort of her own sheets and pillows.

She took one bite of the pizza, then another. She managed to make it through one piece before feeling like she needed to throw up. Maddie fell asleep, not waking up until the morning.

Feeling slightly better the next day, Maddie turned on her phone to see what Melissa had to say about her return. When there were no emails, texts, or missed calls from Melissa, Maddie began to get suspicious. It wasn't like Melissa to not respond, especially to news of Maddie coming home.

After having a cup of coffee, Maddie put on her best pair of sweatpants and made her way to Melissa and Jakob's house. It was still early, but Melissa usually didn't book studio sessions until the afternoon so she expected her to be home.

She pulled in the driveway, then knocked on the door. Steven Tyler came barreling down the stairs to the front door, barking happily at Maddie through the door. Jakob came running down the stairs, and frowned when saw Maddie.

"What are you doing here?" He asked her incredulously as he pulled the door open, his dark beard frazzled. Maddie bent down to pet the giant sheepdog, Steven Tyler, and receive his many kisses. When she stood up, she looked puzzled.

"What are you talking about?"

"You're supposed to be in Scotland!" Jakob said, unnaturally frantic. His deep voice was panicked as he listened to what his beloved fiancé's sister had to say.

"I emailed Melissa an entire day ago and told her I am coming back early," Maddie said, pulling out her phone. She pulled up her email app, looking at her sent messages, and discovered that no email existed. Scoffing, she brought open the drafts folder and found it there. "Damn!" She said, "It didn't send. Well, anyway, where's Melissa?"

"She's in Scotland," Jakob said through gritted teeth.

"What?" Maddie exclaimed. "What are you talking about?"

"Mel was so worried about you," Jakob explained. "First you go over there without telling anybody, chasing after some skinny model, and then we see a picture of some other guy kissing you in front of a castle. When she didn't hear from you, she freaked and booked a flight," he said. "She told me she's not coming back without you."

"No," Maddie said, smacking her forehead with her hand. "This can't be happening. How does she know where to look for me?" Maddie asked, her mind going a mile a minute.

"You told her where you were staying, above some bar?" Jakob said questioningly. "She's planning on starting there."

"You have to tell her to come home," Maddie said, dreading the idea of Melissa walking into O'Shaughnessy's and encountering Nick.

"I'm calling her now," Jakob said, leaving the door open for Maddie to walk in as he stormed off into the living room.

"She's here," she heard him exclaim. Then in a lower voice, he muttered, "Thank fuck." A minute later, he walked into the kitchen. "She's going to board the flight back home," he said. "She figured out pretty quickly that you weren't there anymore."

"I feel like such an idiot!" Maddie said, biting a fingernail for the first time in her life.

"It's okay, Maddie," Jakob said sympathetically. "You know how Melissa is. She likes to watch out for you. Everything will be okay. More importantly," he said grabbing her shoulders. "Are you okay?"

"I will be," she said honestly. After spending a few more minutes at Jakob's house, Maddie went back to her apartment. Since she was back early, she decided to shower and go into work. She missed the library, her coworkers, and all the children.

After the initial hullabaloo when she first returned, Maddie quickly fell back into her routine. She counted down the hours until Melissa would return, hardly knowing what she was going to say when she saw her again.

Maddie realized that she should have known she was doing the wrong thing when she did not want to tell her sister the truth. Regretting her decisions, Maddie realized that there was not much to do anymore but move on and hope that Melissa was not too disappointed in her.

Jakob planned to pick Melissa up at the airport the next day, and Maddie wanted to be there when she got home. Maddie sat at their front window with Steven Tyler, waiting rather impatiently for the roar of Jakob's truck.

When she heard it coming down the road, she could practically feel her heart in her throat. She was so nervous to face her sister and to admit that she was wrong, but was definitely more than willing to do so. Maddie watched as Jakob gingerly helped Melissa out of the truck. She looked exhausted, but happy.

When she walked through the door, Melissa said nothing but walked over to her sister and wrapped her in the biggest hug. "Don't ever do that to me again," Melissa chastised, hugging her harder.

"I won't. I'm so sorry. I—" Maddie began, before Melissa's shushing stopped her.

"I don't need to hear it. I understand everything, Maddie. You just take the time you need to do what you need to do, okay? And never leave the country without telling me again." Melissa leaned in to place her forehead on Maddie's and the sisters smiled at each other.

"I promise," Maddie said softly. Maddie was freaked. This was not like Mel. Where was the lecture? The shouting? The crying and shaking because of her concern? Maddie felt like a kid who just got away with something without a grounding.

"Did you talk to anybody there?" Maddie asked, mortified.

"Huh?" Melissa asked, as if that was the most shocking thought.

"How did you find out I wasn't there?" Maddie asked.

"Oh," Melissa said, walking over to the couch. "Jakob called me just as I got off the plane. I didn't leave the airport," she said with a laugh. A wave of relief flooded over Maddie. She was so glad that she didn't run into Nick. How awkward that would be—Melissa running into her "tour guide." *Eek.*

The sisters spent the rest of the night on the couch, talking about everything but Scotland. When Melissa went to the bathroom to throw up, she insisted that she just caught a bug from the plane. Maddie looked at her skeptically, not so sure that was entirely accurate.

Maddie threw herself back into work, ignoring the dreams about Scotland that woke her up in the middle of the night. She insisted that she would get over it—over him—and vowed to do so sooner rather than later.

That weekend, when Maddie suggested that they all go out to the local sports bar with Shannon for beers, Melissa finally caved and told Maddie that she was two and a half months pregnant. Instead of going out, they spent the weekend online shopping for baby clothes, nursery furniture, and everything else under the sun. By the end of the weekend, Maddie knew more about baby bottles than she ever thought was possible.

There was nothing better to take her mind off of Nick than focusing on the future baby in the family. When she wasn't working twelve hour days at the library, Maddie spent time with Melissa and Shannon. Melissa and Jakob were over the moon excited about the baby and wanted to get married even more quickly. They even talked about just going to the courthouse one Friday instead of making it into a big to-do. Maddie secretly hoped that they would do a little something more, but kept her opinion to herself.

The morning of Valentine's Day, Maddie was in her office. She wore a black pencil skirt and fitted blazer, a puffy red blouse poking out from underneath. Her red heels matched the blouse. Although she was miserable, she at least wanted to attempt to look cute.

She was on the phone with a children's performer and slammed the phone down when one of her clerks came rushing into the office. "What?" Maddie snapped. She was usually a friendly person, especially at work, but found herself incapable of keeping her temper in check ever since coming back from Scotland.

"I am busy right now," Maddie chastised the poor clerk. "I almost scheduled the Danny Doughnuts performance at the same time as the Family Fun Festival," she screeched, nearly hysterical.

"I'm so sorry to bother you right now, Maddie," the bumbling clerk said, fighting through the words.

"There's a man in the rare books room with a dog. We don't know what to do."

"Is it a service dog?" Maddie asked, her face burning with rage.

The clerk nervously shook her head, then ran back out to the front desk. Maddie cursed under her breath, then stormed out of her office. The clerks murmured nervously as Maddie stormed to the back of the library, her heels clicking as she walked.

She opened the glass doors of the rare books room and shut them behind her. A man stood with his back to her, a small black Scottie dog on a leash next to him.

"Sir," Maddie said exasperatedly. "If your dog is not a licensed service dog, there is no exception to our rules and your dog is certainly not welcome in the rare books room," she continued. Maddie had no patience for this kind of behavior today. She highly doubted a Scottie dog puppy was this man's service dog.

When the man did not turn around, Maddie continued. "Sir, did you hear what I said?" she asked. The man's back stiffened, and he turned around slowly.

There, in front of her in the rare books room of the Willow Falls Public Library, stood Nicholas O'Shaughnessy.

Chapter 18

"What are you doing here?" Maddie asked, wondering if she was perhaps going into shock, or maybe going crazy.

"I'm so sorry," Nick said, his brogue stronger than ever. Maddie shook her head, willing to unhear it. She spent weeks trying to forget Nick's voice, and here he was, letting it all come rushing back to her.

"There's nothing to say," Maddie said quietly. She was so hurt by what he did that she was unsure if there was anything that Nick could say to mend her broken heart.

"Please, let me talk," Nick said. "I have made many mistakes in my life. You know about most of them now," Nick said. "The biggest mistake, though, was leaving you behind that morning. I was a fool, and if you'll have me, I would like to spend the rest of my days trying to make it up to you."

Maddie took a step closer to Nick, captivated by what he had to say. Nick took that as a sign to continue, and took a step forward himself.

"Mum told me that she told you about Elliot," he said, standing tall in front of her. He wore his typical jeans and a red flannel. Maddie noticed the deep circles under his eyes. "I should have told you. After everything you told me, it would have been only right. It sounds silly," he said, rubbing his hand on his face, "But I guess seventeen years wasn't long enough time to be ready to talk about it.

"The moment you stepped into the pub, I knew you were different. You're like no woman I've ever seen. Not only are you beautiful, but you're the kindest soul I know. You even gave poor Calum a chance, and that's saying a lot." Maddie smiled at this and waited for him to continue.

"After what happened with Elliot, I didn't think that I deserved anything good in life. I killed my best friend, no matter how unintentional. There were years when I didn't think I even deserved to live," he continued. Maddie's face fell when he said this. She couldn't imagine that pain that Nick went through and she wished that she could have been there for him.

"I haven't felt like that for years, but I've never really felt like I deserved love, certainly not with a woman like you. I couldn't be around someone that I treasure so much only to risk hurting her. My worst fears came true. I tried to fight my feelings for you. It helped knowing that I'm not the type of man you like, but it couldn't keep me away." At this, Maddie made a move to argue with him, her hand going up to disagree. Nick motioned her hand down, and urged her to let him continue.

"But the fact of the matter is that I've loved you since I first set my sights on you, and I've been *in love* with you nearly that long. It has not been long at all since I've known you, but you have completely ruined me for any other woman. It can only be you. I will never forgive myself for hurting you, for trying to pretend like we could be just friends. I should have never left you that morning. A man who has done what I've done doesn't deserve a woman like you." Maddie could hear the regret in his voice, the gravelly tone even deeper than usual.

"What made you come here?" Maddie asked, not understanding or even believing that he was really standing in front of her.

"Melissa," Nick said matter-of-factly. "That's one hell of a sister you have," he said with a smile.

"What?" Maddie practically screamed. The small dog that was next to Nick let out a bark, temporarily bringing Maddie out of her stupor.

"Melissa came storming into the pub a day after you left, holding up pictures that you must have sent her of O'Shaughnessy's with me in the background. She had a picture of us in front of the castle, with me kissing you," Nick said, a blush creeping up on his face.

Maddie's mouth hung open as Nick continued on. "She demanded to know where you were. After I assured her that Calum was out of the picture, she accused me of hurting you, coming back behind the bar to find keys for the basement. She was convinced that I had you locked up down there. She said she knew that I was the same guy in the background of the photos that you sent her of the bar, so she knew where to find you. She said that she had just traveled seventeen hours and was two months pregnant so I better start talking. When I insisted that I didn't know where you were, she threw a glass of water in my face and made me tell her everything."

Maddie couldn't help but let out a laugh at this, knowing that Melissa was the only person who would dare throw a glass of water into Nick's face. She couldn't believe that Melissa had kept secrets of her own this whole time.

"After I talked through everything with her, we had a good conversation. I realized just how wrong I was and I knew that I couldn't let you go. She got back on the plane a few hours later and we had the plan all figured out."

Tears filled Maddie's eyes as she thought about how much work went into this, not only from Nick but also Melissa.

"I know I'll never be like the heroes in the novels you like so much, and I know that I'll never look like how you'd want me to. I can tell you right now that I'll never wear a pair of skinny jeans or a man bun. But I fookin' love you, so so much. And I don't want to let you go." Nick took a step forward, then dropped to one knee. From his jeans pocket, he pulled out a small wooden heart-shaped box. Holding it out in front of her, tears filled Nick's eyes.

"Madeline Rebecca Danzer," Nick began, "Will you give me the ultimate pleasure of being my wife? If you say yes, I promise to work every day of my life to keep you happy in all ways."

Maddie began shaking in her heels as she gazed down at Nick while he opened the box. Inside, a ring with a beautiful antique setting with an oval emerald shimmered in the fluorescent lighting. Dropping down to her knees in front of him, Maddie leaned forward, tears in her eyes. She closed the delicate wooden box, and for a moment, Nick looked heartbroken.

Clutching his hands, Maddie peered into his eyes. "Say it again," she said stoically.

Nick looked confused, then said, "Will you marry me?"

Maddie shook her head. "Not that," she said.

He paused for a moment, then lit up. "I love you. In fact, I fookin' love you," he said, stronger than ever.

With that, Maddie couldn't resist. Leaning forward, she kissed Nick, clutching both sides of his face. "I love you too, Nicholas," she whispered. "Forever."

"And then some," Nick said, smiling at her.

With that, the Scottie began to bark again. "Oh," Nick said, handing the ring box to Maddie while he picked up the dog. Maddie opened the box and slipped the ring on her finger. "That was my great-grandmother's," he said as she gazed at it glowingly.

"It's beautiful," she said.

Nick nodded. "Just like you." He handed the puppy to Maddie. "I got you this puppy, if you'd like him. You wanted dogs, and since I couldn't bring you a highland cow, I figured she'd have to do."

"A puppy? For me?" Maddie said, "Wasn't the ring enough?"

Nick shook his head. "Nothing is enough for my woman. You deserve everything in the world and more.

I figured that, if there was even the one percent chance that you would accept my proposal, we'd have to be away from each other for a bit while we get everything figured out and I take care of selling the pub and finding a job. I didn't want you to be lonely in the meantime."

Maddie snuggled the puppy close to her as she watched Nick incredulously. "You mean you want to come here?" she asked, hardly believing that the Beast turned into the Prince after all.

"Absolutely," Nick said. "We can still go back to Scotland and visit often."

"And the pub?" Maddie asked.

"I'm going to sell it to someone who actually wants to make it better like Elliot did. My parents agree it's the right thing to do."

Maddie nodded. "I'm so damn proud to call you mine," she said happily.

"You have no idea how much that means to me, love. I know it's fast, but I can't imagine my life without you in it," he said.

The puppy barked once more and they both stood up, walking out into the library. Maddie grabbed her jacket as the clerks and her director stood beaming with smiles, clapping as the couple left the library. Snow was just beginning to fall as they walked down the steps, the puppy skipping along in the snow.

"What will you name her?" Nick asked Maddie as they held hands, the beautiful green gem reflecting against the snow on the ground.

Maddie smiled and thought about it for a moment. "I think she looks like a Haggis," she said proudly.

"Haggis?" Nick smiled. "Absolutely not!"

"Not so fast, mister," Maddie said. "The first rule of this engagement is that you don't get to tell me what to do," she teased. She smiled up at him and said, "But I think Nessie fits her a bit better, don't you think?"

Nick looked relieved at the name change, and bent down to kiss her on the cheek before they went off to become reacquainted with each other.

"Whatever you want, little one. Forever."

Hours later, after the news broke, Shannon announced to the entire town that she was throwing a party for the happy couple on Friday night.

Nick and Maddie managed to tear themselves from her bedroom to make it to the event on Friday. Shannon's tiny cafe was crowded with people drinking copious amounts of wine and eating a huge Midwestern-style buffet of food.

Loud love songs blared out of the stereo and Melissa and Jakob stood huddled in a corner, his hand lovingly on her stomach.

Maddie didn't know half of the people in the room, and the others she only knew from the library, but she supposed the party guests didn't matter as much as how happy she was to be with Nick. Maddie wore a black dress. Nick donned black pants and a green sweater.

Maddie happily showed off her engagement ring to anybody who wanted to see it, hardly believing that it had been less than two months since she met the love of her life.

Nick and Jakob got along very well, and spent a fair amount of time talking about everything, from the sisters to their crafts. The two were nearly the same height. Maddie remembered Shannon's joke about the two being long lost brothers. Aside from Jakob's dark brown hair in contrast to Nick's sandy brown, the similarities were undoubtedly there.

Jakob smiled at Maddie as he spoke to Nick. When Nick walked away to talk to Melissa, Jakob nodded his approval to Maddie. Maddie was overjoyed.

Melissa looked over to Nick, holding up a glass of water and narrowing her eyes at him. Nick's eyes grew wide as he held his hands up and walked backwards. Melissa threw her head back and laughed, then set the water down. Nick smiled, walking over to his future sister-in-law. If possible, she was even tougher than Maddie.

Shannon introduced Nick to her brother, who owned a construction business in town. The two talked for a while, mostly about different types of wood native to Scotland. Maddie interjected and showed Phil pictures of Nick's woodworking. After scrolling through the pictures of his work, Phil offered Nick a job on the spot.

Nick could hardly believe it and gratefully accepted the offer. He knew that there would be time before he could come back to stay for good, but Phil kept the offer open. Shaking his hand and thanking him profusely, Nick was shocked at the kindness and generosity that the community was showing him.

Maddie and Nick clinked their glasses together as they toasted to their future. She had no doubt that things would only get better from here. She loved Nick. She loved him absolutely unconditionally, just as he did her. Nick would do just about anything to be with her real life hero. Maddie realized that, not only was she Nick's heroine, but she was her own as well.

Epilogue

Shannon carried empty boxes to the dumpster when the party began to clear out at eleven. Her dark bob was pulled up in two ponytails and she maneuvered the boxcutter out of a pocket of her faux fur white cape.

Just as she was about to begin cutting the boxes down, blue and red lights filled up the alleyway. She turned to see a police car carefully coming towards her in the alley, then being put in park.

Shannon turned back around to finish cutting down the boxes. It was too damn cold to deal with Willow Fall Police Department's BS. They usually left her alone, but whenever they bothered her it was always about something pointless.

"Quite a party you have going on in there," a southern voice drawled. She heard the door to the cruiser slam and footsteps crunching toward her in the snow.

After lunging the boxes into the dumpster, Shannon tucked the cutter back into her cape and turned around. This was no Officer Dick, the seventy-five year old who had been patrolling the big, bad streets of Willow Falls for at least forty years. Dick was used to her issues with authority, and knew when to take a step back and let her cool down.

Instead, Shannon came face to face with a tall brute of a man. She could have sworn that with one wrong move, his arm muscles would shred his uniform shirt to pieces. The man, who must be around her age, had long, light brown hair, but trimmed on the sides. Shannon squinted at him. She had never seen him before, she was certain of it.

She hated being alone with men, especially when she didn't have her pepper spray on her. She stood back, attempting to catch her balance in case she needed to kick his shins and pop him in the groin.

"Yes, just winding down," Shannon said before going to slam the dumpster shut.

"Looks like alcohol is being served in there," he continued to drawl, hooking his fingers into his police belt. "Do you have a license for that?"

Shannon could have sworn that the guy was getting off on interrogating her. In a huff, she walked back to the door, swinging it open. "It's a private party," Shannon said assertively. "Afterhours."

"I see," the officer continued. "Well just make sure that it stays private, okay ma'am?" he said.

"I really don't need to hear your threatening, hypermasculine bullshit tonight," Shannon said. "I know you don't know who I am, but I am a respected business owner in this town and I refuse to be talked down to by a man whose name I don't even know."

The man's eyes sparkled in the security light of the alley. "Oh?" He said. "So you want to know my name, do you?"

"I would, actually, and your badge number, too," Shannon said.

He had to laugh at that. In a small town like this, there was only one person with a badge. After a moment, he said, "Kennedy, badge number 438549. What's yours?"

"Shannon Romano," she said sternly. "Badge number FK -ZERO- FF." With that, she slammed the metal door behind her and locked it, shutting off the security light.

Benjamin Kennedy stood in the dark alley, only lit up by the lights from his squad. *Shannon Romano*, he mused. He thought about the captivating woman as he walked to the car, sporting a grin from ear to ear. She was going to be a handful.

The End

About the Author

Jacqueline Francis is a small-town Librarian from Wisconsin. She has been fascinated with romance novels since she was a teenager. When not dreaming up swoon-worthy fictional men, she likes to read about them! Find out about what she is reading by following her on Instagram, @jackiereadsromance. *Returning His Love* is her second novel.

Made in the USA
Monee, IL
02 February 2020